I0548412

THE
SIGN OF
THE END

TIMOTHY W. AYERS

This is a work of fiction. Names, characters, places, and incidents are products of the author's imagination or are used fictitiously and are not to be construed as real. Any resemblance to actual events, locations, organizations, or persons, living or dead, is entirely coincidental.

World Castle Publishing, LLC
Pensacola, Florida
Copyright © Timothy W. Ayers 2016
Paperback ISBN: 9781629894263
eBook ISBN: 9781629894270
First Edition World Castle Publishing, LLC, February 15, 2016
http://www.worldcastlepublishing.com
Licensing Notes
All rights reserved. No part of this book may be used or reproduced in any manner whatsoever without written permission, except in the case of brief quotations embodied in articles and reviews.
Cover: Timothy Ayers
Editor: Maxine Bringenberg

Now as He sat on the Mount of Olives, the disciples came to Him privately, saying, "Tell us, when will these things be? And what will be the sign of Your coming, and of the end of the age?" — Matthew 24:3

PROLOGUE

Beth, my wife, is clutching the broken forms of our grandchildren. They are all dead a few feet above me. Beth threw herself over the children in an attempt to protect them from the falling debris of the house. Their mother, my daughter, is somewhere under the rubble of our mountain home. Their deaths were quick.

I'm trapped in a pocket under the rubble. I had gone down to the basement to gather my notes and files. At that point, I was still undecided. Should I print what I know? A whisper of me unveiling the truth had put my family in our mountain hideout. One option was to burn the last of the proof, and to live quietly in the pain of knowing that somehow the world's end had its beginning in me. My name is Matthew MacDonald. I used to be a good bio-geneticist and a good husband. Now I'm neither.

The earthquake had come without warning, devastating every home on the mountainside. For a while after it hit, I heard an occasional moan coming from nearby piles of wood and rock. Those who survived their houses collapsing faced the terror of dying from starvation underneath their once comfortable homes. I should be weeping for them and my family. Instead, I am writing. I can't stop writing. As I scribble these notes, I can see out of the hole I've dug in the side of the rubble. It is my light and my air.

Nothing much is left. How did we in California ever think the colliding faults of the world would somehow miss us? The quakes started in Eastern Europe, and then Japan was ripped open. Long dead volcanoes spit up their molten guts into the seas, spoiling and poisoning most of the water. At times, noon was like midnight when the sun was covered by the heavy volcanic ash drifting through the air. I knew it wasn't long until California would crack as well. But we couldn't leave. Our family had no choice in the matter. Prayers became our only protection. Possibly my family's quick death was the final answer to our heavenward whispers; I don't know. At this point, I know little except that what I have to say may bring some sanity back into a world that is spinning on an axis of madness.

I'm compelled to tell my story. But what I'm writing isn't easy to believe. As you read this, open your mind to the fact that not everything is as it appears. Not everything comes from the source you think it's coming from.

The people I'll tell you about are not what you think. In fact, they may be the opposite of everything they say. I've spent years watching and talking to them. I've gathered my notes from various news magazines, papers, biographies, journals, and a misplaced diary. Before returning it I made a photocopy, which has proven very valuable. I also had two other sources from deep inside their circle. In one case, only a few people could know and tell me what they have. In the other case, the letters are simply signed "Faithful."

I'm writing because I've got to stop them. Somehow I need to survive. I've been able to gather a few salvageable cans of food and bottles of liquid from the rubble of our basement. I pray I make it out alive. If I don't, then I ask that whoever finds my words can put an end to what, I'm sorry to say, I started. Whoever you are that is reading this — let the world know what is contained here. I caution you, if you do, prepare to be hunted. For they'll stop at nothing.

...and the whole world lies under the sway of the wicked one. — I John 5:19

CHAPTER 1

It was nearly thirty-four years ago that Father John Russo, an American priest attached to the Vatican, walked into my laboratory in Zurich, Switzerland. Russo had moved quickly up the ranks of the priesthood. Born in Chicago, he made easy connections with the financial director of the Archdiocese of Chicago. The Chicago diocese had been suspected of passing underground funds through the Vatican bank for laundering purposes. Russo attended St. Mary's Seminary in Mundelein, IL, where he met Monsignor Callahan. The aging Callahan was the primary contact for underworld money. The old man liked something in the seminary student Russo. Maybe it was the same thing that he saw in himself when he stared in the mirror. It was that "do whatever you have to do to reach your goals" look. Once Russo graduated, Callahan brought the new priest onto his staff.

In a few years, the Vatican bank needed a new financial director. The last chief of Catholic finances had run into an "accident." Callahan was the logical choice. He already knew where the money came from, and he simply would work now on the receiving end, the laundering process. Callahan had brought his most trusted aid, John Russo, to Rome with him.

Father Russo did well inside the sacred walls of the pope's domain, often debating theology and social matters with the pontiff himself. The youthful priest rose quickly, but had wanted it to be faster. He had set his sights on his goal—to be the Vicar of Christ, the pope. Russo knew every pathway, every pitfall, and looked for all avenues to fulfill his dream. But it wasn't until he read my doctoral thesis that his vision cleared and he set his direction. In his diary he wrote, "It is an idea that would bring me to the pinnacle of power within the Roman Catholic Church." It was from his diary, mistakenly left behind in my office years later, that I discovered the real Father Russo and the thoughts behind the man.

I remember our first meeting clearly. Father Russo's olive-skinned, slight form moved gracefully toward me as he extended his thin, tight hand. "I'm Father Russo. Your lab assistant said I'd find you in here. You are Dr. Matthew MacDonald, aren't you?"

"Yes. How can I help you, Father?" I felt tense, like in the old days at Catholic school when a priest walked into the room. There was always a sense of nervousness, and the lingering question, "What did I do wrong?" I had continued my association with the church after college and into grad school. Even while working on my doctorate, I had never given up on the church. Lots of my friends had left to search for what they called "the truths of life." Instead, they found themselves chasing after mammon while letting their faith evaporate. In my mind, I saw the connection between my work as a genetic engineer and the works of God as a genetic designer. Of course, if the Vatican had known that I was writing my thesis on cloning a human being, they wouldn't have been overjoyed with their Catholic educated biologist.

I watched as Russo guided his gaze along my reddish face. His diary's entry read that he knew there was something inside my young scientific mind that could help revolutionize the religious world, or at least refocus it to fit his plans. I noticed how different we looked from each other. My form, with reddish blond hair and a slightly freckled face, towered over the dark-skinned priest.

We shook hands and Russo spoke again. "Dr. MacDonald, I'm with the Vatican. We are investigating the theory of cloning, and I wondered if you could explain the process to me."

I was preparing a slide for the microscope, and as was my procedure I set it meticulously aside before answering. I was being cautious and this gave me the time to think. I wondered if the pope considered it a mortal sin to believe and experiment with cloning. I decided that I needed to be careful of what I said. When I spoke again, I asked Russo, "That's not an easy task. Do you have any particular questions on the matter?"

"Actually, I do. I read in your thesis that you believe that cloning a human from DNA samples is possible. I was wondering, is it just theoretical or is it really possible?" the priest quizzed.

I was concerned. Was the pope angry over my thesis? Was there a possibility of excommunication? I rarely held back my thoughts so I blurted out, "Am I in trouble with the pope?"

Father Russo laughed, turning his mouth's corners up and then opening it widely so his white teeth could accentuate the humor of my question, and the harmlessness of his own query. Russo swung his arm around my shoulder and pulled me to a slouch. "No, no. I guess I'm being a little vague here. I have a very special situation, and I'm trying to find the right biologist to assist me in fulfilling the wishes of the Holy See." Father Russo continued. "It seems that you've done ample research on its plausibility. Please, don't fear my questions. I'm sure I can pass on from the Vatican that you are appreciated as one of the brightest young men to come out of our educational system." Russo paused and must have noticed that disbelief covered my face, so he spoke again. "Maybe this isn't a good time to talk. May I come back tomorrow?"

"I guess so. I've already put in too many research hours this week, at least my wife thinks so. You pick the time and we'll get together, but I would prefer that it would be soon."

"What about breakfast? Say about 9 a.m. at my hotel?" Father Russo scrawled the address, shook my hand, and left. I was puzzled but my scientific curiosity was definitely sparked. I hung my lab coat on the hook behind my door and turned off the equipment and lights. I was still thinking about the conversation as I headed home. My car tooled through the streets of Zurich and arrived at the small apartment that the Amrich Corporation had found for my pretty wife and me nearly a year before.

My work on the thesis seemed so long ago. I knew my concepts would work. All I needed was the equipment and time to work out a few variables. Amrich talked about funding the project somewhere in the future. In corporate talk, that meant "don't hold your breath." I tried to convince them that once the DNA code was deciphered, it was simply a job of replacing the DNA of a fertilized human egg with the new code. And bang, you would have it—a clone with the original DNA of another being. The equipment to do this didn't exist then, but I had already designed it.

If only the Amrich Corporation would've supported me on this. I wanted desperately, too desperately, to have the opportunity to perform the experiment, but there were two limitations—money and lab space. Lab space I could find, but the money? Well, on my salary, and with the living expenses in Zurich, I was not able to afford it.

As I reviewed the process, my car seemed to pull automatically into the driveway. My wife, Beth, a beautiful, thin-waisted blonde with deeply expressive eyes, was always worried that I'd have an accident while in this Jerry Lewis Nutty Professor mode. It was not that I wasn't careful, but on this one subject of cloning this scientist was almost possessed. My last thought before entering the house was, If I get the opportunity to clone a human, then where does the money come from?

Beth had started to clean up the dinner dishes when I walked through the door. I remember her sweet, laughing smile as she said, "Let me try to guess. This time you were almost done with the experiment when one of the chimps escaped, grabbed a secretary, climbed up the side of the building, and you had to save the whole world from destruction."

"How do you know what happens at work before I tell you? Do you have a camera in my lab? I smiled back and brushed her cheek with a kiss. We had an understanding. A tense one, but still it was an understanding. Dropping my black tweed overcoat on the antique chair in the hallway near the staircase, I kept talking to her as my ever-present briefcase and I went into the kitchen, "Actually, I got the most interesting visitor today. I almost felt like I was back in Catholic grade school."

"Who was it, Sally Field, *The Flying Nun?*" It was Beth's humorous attempt at keeping up with my incessant referencing of old TV shows. She always thought it unusual that I, a Mensa member, stuffed my mind with more TV trivia than any other baby boomer in the U.S. And she said that to me, often.

With a smirk, I barely acknowledged her attempt at humor, and went on with my story. "No, it was a priest named Russo. He's out of the Vatican. Can you believe that, a Vatican priest? And he came all the way up here to see me."

Beth's interest was raised. I still remember how her soft slippers sounded like satin on our hardwood kitchen floor when she crossed to sit near me at the table. When she sat, I continued. "He had read my doctoral thesis on cloning."

"What? Someone actually reads those things?" she exclaimed with a mixture of surprise and cynicism.

"Yeah, I guess they do. He wanted to know if I could actually do what I said in the paper. Yeah, if I had the—"

Beth finished the statement. "...lab and the money. Does it seem like this Father Russo is serious? Do you think the Vatican wants you to clone someone for them? Maybe one of the popes? You know, after the loss of that earlier one so soon after being elected, maybe they're trying to protect themselves. Kinda like in the movies where they have a stand-in. Like a body double." Her fast paced, rattling speech demonstrated her excitement.

"I don't know, but I plan to meet with him tomorrow morning for breakfast. I'll see then what he wants. And speaking of food, I am starved. Have you and Cari eaten already?" My hunger moved me to the refrigerator. As I yanked on the door, Beth moved up behind me with a warm plate from the oven. "Matthew dear, are you looking for something?" When I turned, she planted a firm kiss on my mouth and handed me the plate.

We continued to talk about the small items of the day like Cari's cute little actions, the mail, and in particular, the letter that had come from my old college friend, Mary Grace. But my mind was still on the earlier meeting, and the one coming the following day. I wondered if I could really do what I'd spent years developing in theory. Somewhere in the back of my mind there was a fear. It rarely showed, but Beth could see it. Then again, she used to see everything that went on inside me. She watched my eyes as I ate and talked. Later, she admitted that she also wondered if I could do everything I'd written about? Was it possible?

TIMOTHY W. AYERS

Be sober, be vigilant; because your adversary the devil walks about like a roaring lion, seeking whom he may devour. — I Peter 5:8

CHAPTER 2

As Beth and I were talking, according to entries in his diary that I later saw, Russo recorded these words in a hotel room on the other side Zurich, Switzerland.

Tuesday, March 28. Once again I am staring at my glass bottle and the small bloody fibers. The fibers look old and brittle. I hold in my hands a true religious relic with enough miraculous power contained within its molecules to bring the nations to their knees. I understand this power. This is the power I've needed.

I remember the Chicago incident again. How they left me twisting in the wind to take the blame. When the investigation occurred, I was left unprotected. The monsignor from Chicago, who directed the Vatican's banking operation, knew that, as a young priest, I would only get a slap on the wrist. The investigators said that I was simply stupid about the monies I accepted. They all thought it would be quietly dismissed. The monsignor had no idea what it did to me. Actually, he didn't care what destruction would come to me. All he cared about was covering his own exposed behind. Tonight, as my eyes study my clear glass bottle, I'm thinking, 'God, I know you understand. I

17

gave everything to your church. I compromised my being for her. Thank you, God. Together, we will get even.'

I feel strange as I write tonight…I feel tired, yet I feel empowered. Something is strengthening me. It must be my holy faith. Much to do tomorrow. Need sleep.

***

When morning came for me, my anticipation seemed to throw my body from the bed. A million thoughts ran through my head. I wondered where I'd order the lab equipment. What about the egg once it was produced? Who would carry the child to term? How much contact would I have afterward?

At that time, I imagined the papers I'd write for the journals and the conference speaking to be done as the first man to clone another human being. I showered, dressed, and was about to leave when Beth came down the stairs. She smiled and said she hadn't seen me like this since the night I asked her to marry me. She told me that I still had all the idealism of a boy.

"Come have a cup of coffee with me before you leave," she said. As she filled our cups, her eye caught the brisk movement of a thick, murky shadow across the floor. Her eyes snapped to the window to see what had glided between her floor and the sun. She blinked. The blind was closed. A shiver ran through her body, creating goose bumps and raising the hairs on the back of her neck. At first, she tried to shake it off with a flip of her hair, but it grew into a deep, disquieting fear. Then she said, "Matt, I'm frightened. Something doesn't seem right. I feel like we should pray, but first let me tell you what I saw."

I felt a strange after she finished. "Okay, Beth. I'll pray." It had been so long since I had prayed out loud, and for some reason the "Our Father" or "Hail Mary" didn't seem right for this occasion. I wasn't very practiced in the art of heavenly communication, and I was surprised when out of my mouth blasted these awkward words: "Lord, help us!" Our fear subsided. Cari must have been startled by my prayer and woke up. Her cry kicked Beth into her daily routine, and I bolted out the door for my meeting with Father Russo.

On the other side of town, Father Russo must have risen early, as he had several letters in his hand as he approached me. One was to an internationally known television evangelist who went by the name Prophet T.N. Thompson. I noticed the address when he dropped the letters in the mail box as we met for breakfast.

At that time I knew nothing of this Thompson, but soon we'd be colleagues. It wasn't until his authorized biography was published that I read his story. A source close to him told me the truth behind the book's script. Thompson had risen from a small Florida church to be one of the earliest and most recognized religious figures on television. The Florida days stayed fresh in the prophet's mind. He remembered those lean times, and that Sunday night service when Laura Severson came forward for prayer.

To the world, the Holy Ghost spoke to the prophet. Those closest to him knew it was a low, reverberating male voice that started to speak inside his head. At first he ignored it. Thompson thought that he was just extremely tired. The little church kept him jumping seven days a week. The church's slow growth left the deacon board with little money to hire more help, and lots of work to be done. Most of it fell to Reverend Thompson, as he was called then.

It was when he had neared exhaustion that Thompson experienced the voice. It had begun when he was a teen, but it came rarely then. Thompson barely remembered it, according to the biography. He tried not to remember much of his childhood. His parents had made that easy. The reverend wanted to force from his mind the memories of their abuse and alcoholic rages. But on that night the voice told him something about Laura.

She had asked to be forgiven. Laura confessed that she had grown to hate her husband. Willy Severson was an alcoholic who often beat Laura. She had turned to the church for support and some answers. Thomas Nigel Thompson rarely had any of the answers she needed or wanted. But that night the voice spoke about Laura. *Laura's husband will die after complications caused by an accident*, the voice stated. Thompson had fought the urge to speak those words to her. Several thoughts went through his mind. *What if I am wrong? What if it really is my typical Sunday evening energy drain that is causing this?* He hadn't felt exhausted though. It was just the opposite. It felt more like his entire body pulsed with electrical current.

He tried to shake it off. He couldn't. *The voice came back again. Her husband will die after an auto wreck. Tell her those words.* He struggled, but finally the voice overpowered him. T.N. Thompson spoke to her as he gripped her head between his hands. He lowered his own head and spoke into her ear. It was nearly inaudible.

"What was that, Reverend? I didn't hear you," Laura said.

He spoke louder. "Your husband will die in an auto wreck. As we pray together he is out drinking. On his way home, a pickup truck will run a red light, pinning him in the car. Two days from now he'll die."

Thompson was stunned when Laura called the next day to ask him to meet her at the hospital. Her husband had been drinking and got into an auto accident. The doctors didn't expect him to live. Reverend Thompson spent many hours consoling her in, as she called it, "special ways" after that. Laura continued her support and ministry to his needs as his personal secretary and assistant.

When the news of the prophecy spread, more people came to that little Florida church building each evening to hear the prophet and to have him prophesy over them. The collection plates filled to the top as they passed through the unpadded, cracked pews. Books were written. Television programs were produced. And before Thompson knew it, a prophet was born and profit was made. Now, the prophet T.N. Thompson saw millions of dollars given to his ministry each year.

The deep, masculine echoing voice in his head got stronger, and the lust for the unholy trinity of money, power, and flesh strengthened. Something great was about to come, the voice said. A few days after I met with Russo, the voice gave the prophet this message: *Look for the priest. Look for the priest.*

...for the ruler of this world is coming... — *John 14:30*

CHAPTER 3

As Russo dropped his letters into the mailbox, we shook hands and entered the restaurant. "Good morning, Dr. MacDonald. I'm glad you could make it. I have so many things I want to go over with you," the priest said through his grinning teeth.

I was more than glad to be there. The young Vatican attaché just might be my ticket on the train to science history and to the top of my field. Working for Amrich had been profitable, but nothing would compare to finalizing my greatest project—my dream. I knew I'd do anything to make it a reality.

"Father Russo, I could hardly sleep thinking about our conversation yesterday," I said as I turned and took my seat.

"Good, because I hope what I have to say this morning will stir your scientific mind to a new height, and in turn we can form a union that will bring about peace to this world." Russo was interrupted by the waiter. He ordered and returned to his conversation. "As I asked yesterday, can you really clone a human being from DNA?"

I'd always relished any chance to explain my thesis. I talked rapidly and animatedly about my favorite subject, and then summed it up. "In short, Father Russo, it can be done. But it will take a lot of money, and I'll need an outside lab to work in. I've got a commitment to Amrich that I can't break, so this will need to be done in the evenings and weekends."

"How long?" asked Russo.

"Maybe two or three months. Do you realize it could cost close to two or three million for us to clone just one egg? Then we need to find someone willing to carry it to term," I stated.

"Those will be my problems. I should have the money in another month. Then we'll begin," the priest answered as he sipped his coffee. "Now, I've got to ask you something."

"What is it?"

"Who have you told about this?"

I twinged and answered, "Only my wife."

"Good. Keep it that way, because this is totally secret. I want no one to know about your work. Tell your wife nothing else from this point on," instructed Russo with a hushed, serious tone.

"Okay," I agreed, but somewhere inside me was an unfounded yet nagging suspicion. I looked down at my coffee as if it were more interesting than our conversation, thought for a moment, raised my gaze, and asked, "Are you sure this is on the up and up? Where does the pope fit into this?"

"The Vatican is totally behind it, but they want no one to know. This is far too sensitive an issue. It's extremely important, and we don't want some kind of public outcry to stop the project before we begin. That can happen, you know. It must be kept secret at all costs. We'll make the announcement when the time comes." Russo stared at me intensely.

I was frightened and jokingly said, "It sounds a little more like a *Man From U.N.C.L.E.* TV show than a scientific endeavor."

The priest put down his fork. "Son, your church needs you. We may create the answer to the world's ills in the next few months. The pope, the Vatican, and the clergy around the world are counting on what you'll be doing."

"All my life I've wanted to be a good Catholic. I feel as though I have little choice in this matter. If my church needs me, I'll go through with it, but let me repeat, it will cost a lot," I stated, with emphasis on the cost of the project.

"For a project of this magnitude, money will be no object. We must have it done, and it must be done quickly." Father Russo unlocked his leather briefcase and pulled from its pockets a glass bottle. "This bottle contains the DNA. I'll turn it over to you when the lab is ready. Now, you need to give me an idea of how much money you would like for doing this."

I was flip and threw out a figure. "A million." I thought the amount would show the priest's cards. It didn't happen.

"It's done," Russo answered.

"That simple, huh?" I was still smiling from my new million dollar salary, and jokingly asked the priest, "You're willing to put all this money up for one experiment. Who is it we're trying to clone—Jesus?"

Without moving his coffee from his lips, Russo answered, "Yes."

TIMOTHY W. AYERS

...and with him the false prophet who worked signs in his presence, by which he deceived those who received the mark of the beast and those who worshiped his image.
— *Revelation 19:20*

CHAPTER 4

I sat frozen by the shock of the answer. "C'mon. You've got to be kidding. Don't you realize that I need some type of DNA sample that actually belonged to the person before I can clone them? I can't clone Jesus. Where in the world are we going to get DNA from Jesus? I'm a scientist, a biologist, not some kind of miracle worker." My staccato statements peppered the priest.

Father Russo only smiled. He fingered his bottle for a moment, then began to speak. "In this bottle there's—"

"There's just a bunch of strings." I was animated in my disappointment as I finished his statement, threw down my napkin, and began to rise. The few people in the restaurant began to look our way. "You're starting to sound like a religious nut. You come into my lab, and you get my hopes sky high that I'm going to finally do the one thing I've been waiting for, and then you tell me I'm going to clone—"

Russo held up his hand, facing the palm towards me. "Stop, don't say it. I want no one to hear the next few words. Give me time to explain. The fibers in this bottle have been tested. They contain enough DNA material to perform the task I've asked of you."

"Okay, but where does the Jesus part come in?" I asked.

The priest sucked in a breath. I could tell that he knew he needed explain this correctly or the whole project would fizzle. I was, most likely, the only scientist that could do the cloning, and at that point I was anything but happy. Russo held the bottle in the air, twisting it like some type of holographic visual aid. "The cloth these fibers are from came from the body of Christ. When the Lord died, Joseph of Arimathea and others took His bloody body and prepared it for burial. They were in a hurry and had to wrap His form without ceremonially washing it, before the sun went down and their Sabbath began. When He was wrapped in the cloth it soaked up His blood, leaving enough DNA code for you to work with."

I sat quietly, listening to Russo finish his pointed explanation. "That burial cloth is the same one that was left behind when Jesus rose from the dead. It was so indelibly marked by his powerful transition back to life that it has his image fused to it."

I started to track with the priest. I spoke again, displaying interest. "You mean these threads are from the Shroud of Turin? But how in the world did you get these? I mean, that is a religious relic. I can't imagine the curators of that museum in Turin are going to let you walk in and cut fibers from the Shroud."

"You're right, Matthew. If you, as a good Catholic, were to walk in and ask to see the Shroud privately and take fibers to test, you would be refused. Now, if you were an attaché of His Holiness, closely connected to the Vatican, with all the right papers and credentials, you could walk in and take away what you wanted," answered Father Russo.

My emotions were on a wild up and down roller coaster ride. After hurtling downward a few minutes before, I was racing back up with the realization that Russo was not a demented priest that should be locked away. He looked to be a wise and powerful comrade. "I'm sorry, I didn't understand. Forgive me for speaking so quickly and not giving you a chance to explain. I've got to say that I'm still a little taken back by this. Cloning Jesus Christ is a more than I bargained for. It's possible, but is it right?" By this point, I had lowered my voice to a near whisper.

Russo smiled widely and said, "This has already been discussed by theologians within the Vatican. Rest assured that this project has the total support of Rome."

According to Father Russo's diary entry, I later learned this was a lie. Only a month before our meeting, Russo was escorted into the chambers of His Eminence. The pope had barely looked up before he began to launch his tirade. "My dear, young Father Russo...." The diary recorded their discussion. "In the last year, you have been caught in a major financial scandal that has brought great disgrace to the Church, to your fellow priests at the Vatican, and to me. I personally realized that you were simply a pawn being used by others, much like the Jewish scapegoat spoken of in the Holy Word. Because of that, I asked that you be kept on here until we could find the proper assignment. Now, I've heard that you have visited Turin where the Shroud is kept, and removed fibers for examination. Has anyone instructed you to do so?"

Russo wrote, in his diary, of his intense fear of the real plan being exposed. He scrambled for answers. He'd never expected that the pope would discover it so quickly. Words slipped into his mind and he spoke them. "Your Grace, I realized the importance of this relic to the Holy See. I felt that some impartial examination by scientists, not connected to the Vatican or to the liberal forces that would like to see us lose face again, would be helpful. I was simply attempting to regain your respect and trust. I have brought embarrassment to the Mother Church and now desire to restore my name and calling before the eyes of the faithful. Please, forgive me. I should have spoken with you first, but I was afraid that you would have stopped me."

"You're right. I would have stopped you, and as of this moment I am stopping you. I can certainly appreciate your desire. It shows a truly sincere, repentant heart, but please do not move ahead with a project like this. It can be quite damaging to the Church in the long run. I ask that you destroy those threads. We'll find an assignment for you to sink your teeth into. Something that will help you regain your credibility. Johnny, please be patient, and until then take some time off and travel. See other parts of the world."

I guess his travels had brought him to me and this breakfast. I felt the waitress brush by me. "More coffee, Father?"

"Yes, please." As she left he returned to his conversation with me. "As I was saying, we have the backing of the Vatican, but with one small problem. You may remember the recent scandal over finances at the Vatican Bank?"

I was puzzled and I'm sure it showed. "No, not really."

"Well, it was discovered that large amounts of money were being laundered for the American Mafia through Chicago connections to the Vatican Bank. Because of that, finances for this project must be found outside the Vatican. The fiscal dealings in Rome are being tightly accounted for. Any withdrawal of the amount we're talking about would certainly violate our desire for secrecy," expounded Russo.

"So, what are you going to do?" I asked.

"I have contact with an American television evangelist who, I believe, will be interested in the project. He is doing quite well, financially that is, and I'm sure he will see the potential in this project. Have you heard of the Prophet Thompson? He's got a very big following in the States," John asked.

"I remember him, and you're right, he's got the money. But I'm not sure he's the genuine article. Aren't all TV preachers just charlatans, trying to get people's money?" I rubbed my forehead. This had taken another bad twist as far as I was concerned.

"Do you want an honest answer?"

"Yeah, go ahead. I need a dose of reality here," I shot back.

"No, most of the preachers on TV are not fakes. But does it make any difference? His money can fund the project no matter what. If he's a fake, then one of those TV news programs will expose him and we don't have to worry about it. We'll claim that he was simply a financial backer and that we had no idea of his darker side. Now, if he isn't a fake, then he'll be the perfect partner in this endeavor."

I smiled nervously. I realized that Father Russo had thought this project through. I was uncomfortable and still had many unanswered questions, but I nodded my agreement.

The young priest raised his cup of coffee to make a toast. "To the Messiah clone. May he honor the one I serve," Russo said as I imitated his movement and we clinked cups. A chill ran down my back as I looked into Russo's eyes. I saw something briefly. It was only a flash...more precisely, it was like a blink of dark light, if there was such a thing. I had never seen it in anyone before. The muscles tightened in my neck and a shiver rose up through my spinal cord. At that time I thought it must've been a reflection off the moisture in his eye, from the lights from the old chandelier above our table.

Russo took three slow, deep breaths and stood. It appeared to me that he was attempting to control something inside him. The sighs were raspy, and his exhale had the faint odor of eggs, bad eggs. But I didn't remember him having eggs for breakfast. While he was dropping money onto the table, he spoke quickly. "I'll be back in about a week. Have the list of needs for your lab ready and anything else that is necessary. When I return we'll begin." He turned and dragged himself out slowly, as if he were exhausted.

***

Days later, across the Atlantic Ocean, the prophet Thomas Nigel Thompson was awakened by the voice in his head. According to his biography, it spoke loudly and repeatedly; *Look for the priest. Look for the priest.*

Thompson snapped up from his pillow. He couldn't sleep, but then again most nights were sleepless. He thrashed as if he were wrestling with someone most of the night. His secretary, Laura, often laid next to him observing these sleepless nights. Later, she privately told me that it appeared he was trying to cast off an enemy that grasped him in a choke hold. According to her, it wasn't until he muttered phrases of defeat that he finally rested. That night, Thompson never reached a point of deep sleep. He kept hearing the voice. It kept talking. For the third night straight it said, *Look for the priest.*

When dawn came, Tom Thompson rubbed his face hard, trying to wake up. He pushed on Laura's side, edging her body to the side of the bed. "Hey, are there any priests on my appointment list?"

Laura was very groggy. She thought she heard the word "priest," but wasn't sure. "What's that? You want a priest? Are you turning Catholic or what? You want that Extreme Unction stuff done to you?" she slurred with her morning voice.

Thompson was agitated. He had to know why the voice was saying, *Look for the priest.* "I said, 'Do I have any appointments with a priest?'" He repeated it with generous helping of irritation in his voice.

"I got a letter yesterday from a priest, a Father John Russo. He's a Vatican attaché. He said he'd be in town today and wanted to meet with you. I tossed the letter. I figured we'd turn this nut away. He's probably looking for money for some charity they're running."

"Listen, the moment he comes in, I want to see him. Interrupt whatever I'm doing. I have got to talk with this priest." Thompson was adamant.

"Okay, whatever. Can I go back to sleep now?" Laura asked with a certain amount of frustration and bewilderment.

Tom Thompson rose from bed and went into the shower. The voice quieted as he rubbed his body with soap and the cold blasts of water pelted his tired muscles. By the time he moved out of the shower stall, Laura had made his coffee and had it waiting for him. The voice had left him unable to sleep most nights. If it wasn't for caffeine or other stimulants, Thompson could not have gotten through each day.

He began to feel like himself again. The thoughts of the voice and the priest had left him. His mind went over his appointments and projects as he dressed. By 6 a.m., he was in his silver Jaguar headed for the T.N. Thompson Prophecy and Ministry Center. The large structure sat at the end of a long drive outside of Orlando, Florida. Most mornings, he thought of the impact that Disney had on the area. On the good days, he fantasized about building Prophet World, the first theme park for Christians. On his bad days, he tried to remember the earlier ministry days and their simplicity. As Thompson pulled into his parking space, he switched his focus to ministry duties and entered the building.

The television staff meeting was ending at 10:30 a.m. when Laura interrupted. "Reverend Thompson, Father John Russo is here."

Thompson snapped up. His head spun from rising so quickly, and then the voice began...*Listen, receive, follow.* Tom Thompson rubbed his eyes and gathered himself. "Okay, we'll finish this later. I've been expecting Father Russo and I need to get right to him. And Billy, make sure that we get time on that station in Atlanta. Let me know about that this afternoon."

The television ministry team left as Father Russo squeezed by them in the doorway. "Hi, I'm Father Russo. Thanks for seeing me on such short notice."

"I've been expecting you for several days now."

"How? Your secretary said that my letter just arrived yesterday." Johnny was taken aback.

"That's why they call me Prophet Thompson. Please come in and have a seat. I'm very anxious to hear what you have to say. For some reason I feel like this is very important. So, spill the whole story, and let's see what we can do," Thompson said. He directed the priest to the soft chairs next to the large picture window overlooking several acres of soft green grass and palm trees.

Russo spoke. "I'm not sure exactly where to begin. I'll explain the chain of events and tell you why I'm here. Over a year ago, a doctoral thesis by Matthew MacDonald on the subject of cloning human beings came to my attention. MacDonald claimed he had found a way to clone life from DNA patterns."

The prophet held up his hand and indicated a need to stop the discussion. "Listen, Father, before you go any further. Explain how this cloning stuff works. I'm not a rocket scientist or a biological scientist. I didn't even do well in junior high science. I'm just a backwoods preacher that God has called to touch people's lives." Thompson almost believed the string of half-truths he told everyone.

"I'll keep the process simple since I only understand it on a simple level myself," John began. Thompson smiled, and thought the two would be able to understand each other. The priest continued. "MacDonald uses nano-surgery to remove the nucleus from a body cell and then isolates the DNA code. At that point he can change it to match any code he desires. It's like your garage door opener. If the neighbor is on the same frequency, you just pop it open, flip the switches on the opener, and the remote code is changed. MacDonald does the same thing. Once he's changed the code, he replaces the nucleus. The ovum then develops without fertilization. The embryo then is made up of cells from the new DNA code."

"Okay, I'm with you so far," Thompson said with genuine interest. Even without the voice in his head, Thompson felt there was something intriguing about this. He later revealed that his first reaction was to wonder who in the world this guy wanted to clone.

Russo continued. "I've met with MacDonald. He is absolutely sure he can clone from a DNA pattern. It will take him roughly three months to complete the project."

Thompson was lost. "Who cares how long it will take? What are we trying to do here?"

Father Russo seemed to realize that he was getting ahead of the story and needed to put the conversation back on common ground. "Let me explain. Because of my close connection with the Vatican, I was able to travel to Turin, Italy, where the Holy Shroud is kept. I removed several strands of fiber." Russo pulled the bottle from his case and spun it around in front of Thompson. "These strands were soaked with the blood of Jesus. They give us the original DNA for the Messiah. With MacDonald's expertise, my connections, and your money, I believe we can clone the one person who can change the course of history."

Thompson leaned forward, drawn into Russo's story. There was an eagerness in his spirit and in his voice. "Please, tell me again. Who is it we're going to clone?"

Russo was hesitant, but read the look in the prophet's eyes. "Jesus Christ," he said as calmly as a man ordering lunch.

Thompson almost fell off his chair. The concept was hard to comprehend. To clone Jesus seemed somewhat blasphemous. He was torn between laughing at the priest and jumping on board when the voice began. *Listen, follow, receive, join.* Thompson shook his head to stop the voice, but it only got stronger.

According to his journal, Russo thought he had lost him. He began to pack the bottle away and prepared to leave. He'd find backing somewhere, but Thompson didn't seem to be the one. And yet, he had felt very directed towards this prophet.

As he stood to leave, Thompson stopped him and spoke. "Hold it, don't go anywhere. I'm very interested. I've just got some questions."

Russo sighed as he dropped with relief back into his chair. "Please, ask. I feel like I've gotten ahead here and your questions may clear things up."

"First of all, how do we know this is the DNA of Jesus? There ain't a whole lot of us outside the Catholic Church that believe the Shroud is from Jesus's body," Thompson questioned.

"You're right. There is documentation on this Shroud back to only 1354 A.D. Around the fifth or sixth century, St. Nino, a native of Jerusalem, referred to the burial cloth of Jesus. Around the seventh century there were several references to the Shroud and the imprint that was on it. In 1171 A.D, William of Tyre, who accompanied the king of Jerusalem to Constantinople, said that the Shroud was preserved at the palace.

"The image was like a negative in a photograph, and since this process didn't exist in the early centuries, we can deduce that no one would have been able to predict what a negative would look like. All experiments have proven that there is no sign of it being painted. From this evidence, I assume that this really is the shroud of Christ. Yes, there are some questions as to its authenticity, but the evidence in favor outweighs the evidence against it."

Thompson drew in a breath and exhaled his words. "Suppose it is genuine and you have this DNA, and you have this biologist; then what? Who carries the baby? And what do we do with him, once we have this clone of Jesus?"

Excitedly, Russo spoke again. "I have a young nun in the north of Italy who is willing to carry the child to term. Her name, most fittingly, is Maria. Once the child is born we've got to teach him everything in the Bible. I mean everything. He needs to be able to quote every passage. He must sound like the original Jesus sounded, and think like the original Jesus thought, and—"

Thompson stopped him in mid-sentence, "Wait a second…you mean he wouldn't have all the thoughts of Jesus already?"

"Not at all. This is just a physical clone. Most likely, that's where the similarities will stop," answered Russo.

"So, whatever we feed into this clone is what it will be?" Thompson stated as his mind barreled through the possibilities.

"Yeah. I guess you could put it that way."

Thompson lifted his body from the chair and walked to the window. He was staring at the scenery, smiling. "Father Russo, do you grasp what that means? If the world believes this is Jesus, which he'll be physically, but what he thinks and does is controlled by us, then…well, the world is ours." *The world is ours. Form an alliance, now!* The voice was loud enough to cause Thompson to grab his head.

"Is there something wrong? Are you all right?" asked the father.

"Just a headache. I'll be fine. In fact, I'll be better than fine. I want to form a partnership, now! But I have a few stipulations to add to our deal."

"If they're reasonable I'm sure we can work things out." Russo took in deep breaths and exhaled in rasps. As the prophet had said, "The world is ours."

"I want that baby to come poppin' out on December twenty-fifth, and I want the glorious event to be exclusively televised on my show. Nobody else gets a camera in there. As he grows, I want him on my programs. When he does miracles and wonders, I want those on my shows. The world has got to see me linked with him. I want the world to think of me as the Great Prophet, who speaks for and with Jesus Christ. Is that agreeable with you?"

"I have no problem with that. In fact, I have a feeling we'll be working together for many years. I'm also looking for something out of this."

"It looks like were both in very agreeable moods. What is it?" asked Thompson.

"I want to be the Vicar of Christ." Russo stated his wants quickly.

"The what?"

"Pope, my dear Protestant friend."

"Why not?" The prophet dropped back into his seat, laughing. They looked at each other. Something hellish had connected.

TIMOTHY W. AYERS

For unto us a Child is born, unto us a Son is given; and the government will be upon His shoulder. — Isaiah 9:6

CHAPTER 5

"The media event of the year...that's how Thompson sold this to every cable, satellite, Internet system in America," remarked the lighting crew member to his assistant as they hung the PAR cans and floodlights around the small barn in Bethlehem. Nearly a year after Russo's visit, I stood watching this media event with interest from the background. During college I had done a few theater productions, and the behind the scenes technical work always interested me.

The assistant handed up a red gel for a PAR can. It would be used to warmly tone the skin of the birth mother as the baby was first shown to the world. He asked his boss, "How in the world did he pull this off? First of all, this whole clone sh—I mean stuff—scares the he—heck out of me. And then to work out a deal to televise it from a barn in Bethlehem is unbelievable. This Thompson guy is some kinda wheeler-dealer to pull this off."

Inside my heart, I affirmed that. I was enjoying watching and listening, hearing a different side. This was a side I often missed because I was so close to the event.

The crew chief talked as he worked. "I've been with him for about three years now and he seems to have a knack for this kinda stuff. He knows how to get people interested in what he's doin' and then market it. He's sharp. Give me that wrench over there, will ya? Once I tighten these we need to move to the next support tree, and then that's the last of them."

As the two crewmen finished hanging the lights, I moved near the director, who was checking the "birth of Christ" set. The animals and hay needed to be visible, but not unhygienic. That was what he'd told the set designer. He had to make sure it was done right.

I overheard some of the other workers as they talked. The man who was spreading the hay whispered to the woman setting the blankets in place. "What in the world is he doing in here? He doesn't know anything about health hazards. He's a director." I understood the director's obsession. This was the biggest production he'd ever done. The birth of Christ would be the highest rated TV show in the history of the medium. That would mean one thing to him—moving up to the big time.

While the preparation on the barn took place, I moved over to where Maria was. Thompson and Russo talked with the doctor in the mobile surgical unit. Russo paced like an expectant father while he asked questions. "How long after you induce her will she give birth?"

As the doctor cleaned his hands, he tried to assure the two men that everything was fine. "It won't be that long after I induce, but we'll need to be ready, and we must have Maria in place by that time. I don't want to be moving her when Baby Jesus enters the world. Gentlemen, I suggest you go over there and relax. My medical team can handle this routine procedure from here. That is, if you can call birthing the Christ child routine," he laughed.

Maria laid in her trailer showing the strain of her labor pains. As I looked in on her, I thought about the events that had brought her to that point. We often talked about what was happening in her life. Her honesty and sweetness disarmed me in our communications. Her soft, dark brown hair grew matted with sweat as the make-up people raced about in a flurry of pre-show time activity. They were concerned about her sweet virginal look. It had to be preserved for the camera's sake. The production was being broadcast around the world. In the midst of it, I thought back to what Maria had told me about that first day that Father Russo had gone to the convent.

***

She was a novice, and he had noticed her beautiful, innocent face. Later that day, Russo had asked that the young nun meet with him. After several minutes of getting to know her history, he asked, "Do you love God?"

"Of course, with all my heart and soul and mind."

"If His Excellency, the Pope, were to ask of you a special request, would you be willing to serve him and God?"

"Yes, that is why I have entered the convent. I want to serve my God and my church." She wondered where their conversation was going.

Russo settled back in the austere wooden chair and fixed his gaze upon her face. Russo would often say, "She is perfect. No other could be the mother to the new Christ. Sister Maria was perfect." Russo spoke to her. "Sister, it tells us in the Holy Scripture that our Lord Jesus Christ will return one day and lead his people. That day is not far

43

away. You won't understand much of what I'm going to tell you, but let me go ahead. There is a new scientific process in which we can create an egg from the DNA code of Jesus Christ himself. This egg would be planted in the womb of a virgin, allowing it to grow and finally, into this world a new born baby would arrive. This baby would be Jesus himself."

Maria listened intently. She didn't understand the how, but was willing to obey if she was the one chosen to carry the child. She smiled. I laughed when Maria told me that she thought about how Mary was told by an angel dressed in white. Her angel was a priest dressed in his black suit. It seemed so opposite, almost funny.

Father Russo explained that he wanted her to be the mother that carried the baby, and she nodded. After Russo left, Maria had sat for a while longer, thinking that it must have been a dream. Over the next couple of months, Russo returned several times to talk with her and reaffirm that she was indeed to have the Christ child. It was only a matter of time.

Nine months before this television spectacle, she was brought to Zurich, Switzerland and implanted with the egg. Once the OB-GYN was positive that she was pregnant, Maria was taken to the United States to live in the home of Reverend Thomas Thompson. His secretary, Laura, was her support through the process. Laura was sweet to her as she grew in physical size. Laura would find her clothing. They would go to lunch and shopping. It was a wonderful time. If it wasn't for Laura, she may not have gotten through it all, especially since the pope had removed her from the sisterhood. Thompson tried to keep all news from her, but somehow this one item slipped past. It was on the cover of a newspaper a customer was reading at an eatery in Orlando. His Excellency was not as supportive of the project as Father Russo had said. Then again, that was only the beginning of the falsehoods we were told.

***

The director entered her trailer, swinging the door wide open while barking orders to those around her. As the door continued to move back and forth in the wind on squeaking hinges, the doctors and nurses moved Maria to a gurney. Laura leaned over and kissed her forehead. "I'll be nearby, Maria, praying for you. The moment is almost here. You are blessed."

"Among all women," she grunted out with one of her breaths. Somehow Laura had taken on Elizabeth's role in the Christmas story. If the pains weren't so bad, Maria might have laughed again. That scene left me in tears. These were the only genuine people I met in the entire ordeal.

The director barked, "We go on the air in five minutes. Places everyone. Get that girl into the barn right away, and someone grab that lamb over there before it craps in the barn. Move it out. I like realism, but not that real. Sound! Watch your boom. It's too low."

Amidst this, Maria was wheeled into the barn to become the center of the camera's focus as she delivered the child. The drug she was given to induce labor had pushed the pains to only a minute apart. It wouldn't be long. I saw that she felt the pressure and wanted to bear down, but she knew her technique. She and Laura had gone to natural childbirth classes together. She told me that she knew what to do, but wished that Laura could've been there with her.

The medical teams carefully picked her up and placed her on the table in the barn. "Thirty seconds till show time," the director called out, but the expression seemed out of place for the birth of the Christ child. A voice said, "Ten, nine." Hands fussed with her garments and moved her hair. Make-up had just finished powdering her, but they couldn't control the sweat on her small, beautiful face. Her dark curls fell wherever they wanted. "Three, two — ONE!"

Camera one opened up on The Prophet Rev. T. N. Thompson. A choir sang "O Come All Ye Faithful" somewhere in the background, faintly enough to be heard, but not overpower Thompson's words. He began, "It is after midnight and the start of a new day here in Bethlehem. It is very early in the morning on December twenty-fifth. I'm standing beside a barn behind an inn in the City of David, known as Bethlehem. Nearly two thousand years ago, Jesus Christ was born under the same circumstances to a beautiful young Jewish girl named Mary. He grew to become a man, while all the time holding onto his godhood. This man-god lived amongst his people, teaching them, doing miracles, and prophesying about the future. And at the age of thirty-three he displayed the ultimate act of love — he went to the cross to die for our sins."

The screen faded on Thompson as it moved to an earlier sunset cut of Golgotha hill. The Golgotha set had been erected with a cross jutting out of its crest. To that cross they had affixed a young man; fortunately for him, it wasn't with nails. As the sun rose behind the cross, a silhouette of the figure stood starkly out from the blazing red-orange matte background. The actor raised his head to God and then let it drop. The camera moved in close on his face to reveal bloody, beaten features covered by the rivulets of blood that had flowed out from the crown of thorns. The make-up people had done an excellent job, along with the film crew. They had captured a moving and visually gripping scene for the global TV marketplace. The Golgotha scene cross faded to Thompson's face, superimposed in the same form as the dying Messiah's.

Thompson continued his narrative. "He was placed in a grave not far from the scene of his brutal murder. The grave was carved from the rock, nothing more than a cold, damp, stone cave. Since it was so near the time of the Sabbath, those performing the burial could not take the time to properly prepare the body, so they wrapped him in a shroud. The material soaked up the remains of his blood from the vicious wounds and the many stripes across his back. They remembered the words of the prophets of old, that 'by His stripes we would be healed.' They all went about their religious duties feeling the grief and the loss, wondering what next? They had invested all those years in the ministry of this man who they thought was the Messiah. Now what?

"In those early hours of Sunday morning, the physical body of Jesus Christ went through a tremendous transformation, filled with a heavenly energy that we can't explain. But that energy surged through the shroud, leaving an indelible and mysterious impression as Jesus's body was resurrected. Because of that resurrection, the church has pressed on through the world, making great strides, preaching His message to all men and women. The message of love, hope, and peace.

"Now today, due to modern genetic science, we have the literal body of Jesus being reborn. Not a resurrected, perfect, heavenly body, but a real, flesh and blood body like ours. In that shroud, known today as the Shroud of Turin, the genetic code, or DNA, of Jesus himself was saved and protected over the centuries. Through the hard work of Father John Russo from the Vatican, that DNA code was brought to a biological scientist named Matthew MacDonald. Dr. MacDonald created an egg which was implanted in young Maria. And today, this day, in the City of David, Christ will be reborn."

The scene shifted to the Orlando Prophecy Center's choir, performing "It Came Upon a Midnight Clear." The video technicians had the clip of the Father Russo interview cued and ready. The moment the choir sang their last note the screen faded to Russo.

"It was over a year ago that I first came into contact with Dr. MacDonald. I had just read his doctoral thesis on cloning from genetic material, and it had interested me. As I slept that night, a voice came to me that was far too real to be a dream. Behind the voice was an image filled with light. It told me to seek out Matthew MacDonald, because the time was right for Jesus to be born again on this earth. As an attaché to the Vatican, I was able to gain access to and obtain a DNA sample from the Shroud of Turin. This sample was brought to Dr. MacDonald. From that point I can explain no further, except that Christ the Lord will soon walk this earth again. 'O Come, O Come Emmanuel.'"

The director cut to a commercial. Thompson had realized the worldwide impact of the program, and was able to sell commercials at $1,500,000 a thirty second spot. At that time, it was a great deal of money. Super Bowl commercials were bringing considerably less; but then again, this was the ultimate television spectacular. Every eye in the world would be focused on their television sets.

Coke's "It's the Real Thing" seemed somehow appropriate to Thompson when they bought several minutes of ad time. Thompson drank the product constantly, but he also liked the slogan. The commercial immediately followed Russo's interview. More came along afterward, but Tom Thompson liked "It's the Real Thing." It fit. It said it all with a prophetic tongue in its cheek.

When the commercials ended, the monitors went up with Thompson standing in front of the barn door. It was open and the viewers could see the figure of Maria behind him. Next to her was a doctor dressed in white while he stroked her hair and spoke softly. What he said didn't matter...the scene was for the cameras, not for Maria. Her discomfort meant little to the producers and director. Camera angles were more important than this little angel.

Thompson entered the barn. Camera three came up on him as he walked inside. Thompson turned and spoke over his shoulder into the camera. "In a few minutes, the world will witness the birth of Christ once again. While we wait, contemporary Christian music stars, First Trump, sing their rendition of 'Angels We Have Heard on High.'"

In the background, Mason Sean Blackmore, a record producer, sat watching the whole scene. I overheard him on the telephone saying that he was torn. On one hand, he knew that the music he would release on the New Messiah label would go instant platinum, and probably double and triple after that. On the other side, something was not kosher about all this. When he'd signed the contract, the dollar signs had blinded him. In the months that followed, through his prayer and quiet times, he saw something odd about the situation. He wanted out but couldn't do it. By the end of the phone conversation, Blackmore decided to ride it through. Maybe it was all legit. If it was, he'd enjoy the money. If it wasn't—well, he would cross that proverbial bridge when it spanned the murky, troubled waters.

As the song finished, the word was passed to the director that Maria was ready to give birth. Her labor pains were only seconds apart. The director rushed in and yelled at everyone in the barn to take their places. He looked at Maria and said, "Hold on, sweetie, we've got a minute before the song ends, and then another thirty seconds of intro comments. I'd like to get another two minutes of commercials in if I can. Can she hold back, Doc?"

Maria grimaced in pain. She probably had many words Italian words she would have liked to say to the director. Ones her old Uncle Giordano used to use just seconds before her mother would strike him and say, "Don't use that language in front of the children." Yeah, those were the words she had for the director, I was sure of it.

The director cut for a commercial.

The Spirit Himself bears witness with our spirit...
— Romans 8:16

CHAPTER 6

Across the world television sets were tuned to this miraculous media event. To the religious leaders in the east, a new ascended master was born. To the spiritual awakening in the west, they acclaimed that there would finally be a Jesus with flesh and blood to guide them.

I didn't know the following facts as I watched the birth of my Messiah clone in Bethlehem, but in Vatican City the pope was troubled. He hadn't favored the project from day one. Many of the other bishops had urged him to let Russo continue. They said, "If it's part of God's plan it will happen no matter what. If the new Messiah isn't genuine, the world will reject him." The statement sounded wise. It echoed the words spoken by the Pharisees long ago when the church began. But the Holy Father hadn't agreed with them. He knew that the world waited for a new Messiah. The citizens of earth were desperate for someone to believe in, someone to follow. It didn't make much difference if he was real or not. There was a faith vacuum. The world wanted a Messiah, and Russo and Thompson were giving it to them.

The pope's most disturbing feelings came during his own prayer times. As he touched God, he had no peace about the new Messiah. This unnerved the man who wore the ring of the leader of the Holy Roman Catholic Church. He often prayed, "Give me peace if this is your will." Peace had never come; instead, he saw shadows. From the corner of his eye he saw murky shadows that moved inside of other thick shadows. He saw shadows that cast themselves along walls and floors. There were shadows that came from nothing seen and when nothing was there. One day he would write that he saw shadows that were painted on walls by an unseen artist with a penchant for hellish forms.

***

To the west, across the rolling seas, Brian Guthrie sat with his father, a hospital chaplain, watching the events. Brian had gotten involved with a campus group. Something was ignited inside him. He felt like his faith was real for the first time. It wasn't his father's faith. It wasn't anybody else's faith. This was his own.

The whole Messiah clone topic was hot in their campus group. Most of the others extended wide open arms to a Messiah being born into this earth because of their leader. Brian was a gifted young man that understood spiritual things far beyond his years. Brian was always the first to question any statement that involved God.

Brian sat with his father as the images moved across the screen. Something about the commercials and the big production bothered him. He was interested. Guthrie wanted to see Jesus being born…he wanted to believe this was the real thing. Brian's dad thought it might be a possibility that this was actually Christ. Brian wanted to believe—but he never did. Instead, he watched and wondered what would come next.

***

As the last commercial ended, Maria's contractions came very close together, she couldn't hold off much longer, and she had to push. The camera tightened on her sweet but pained face. Thompson's voice over softly spoke, "During our many centuries of existence only one event separates history into two periods. It draws a line down its center. On one side we denote it B.C. On the other it is referred to as A.D. That world shaking event was the birth of Christ. Will this great miracle, happening at this moment, separate time once again? Yes, you are watching the most important moment of time in our history. The young, virgin mother is ready to give birth. Let's watch this as my Orlando Prophecy Center's Choir sings our most beloved Christmas carol, "Silent Night."

The director whispered to the doctors, "Let her push now. But there isn't any hurry." That was easy for him to say. I could tell from watching Maria that all she wanted was her pain over and done with. The pain stretched her face, her lips drew tight on her teeth, and her jaw clenched hard enough to crack each tooth. She pushed with excruciating pain, and the choir sang with the ease of angels. I wondered if Maria could hear the music. Could she really be giving birth to the Christ-child? It didn't seem possible that a young nun from northern Italy could be lying in a barn in Bethlehem on December 25th and giving birth to the Messiah. Yet, even the Virgin Mary stored words up in her heart because of her own confusion. I remember somewhere in the Bible that she came to Jesus after he had started his ministry and tried to

53

persuade him to stop. Even she was unsure as to his real identity. At least Maria knew it was Jesus.

The doctor called out that the head was visible. Her face showed that it hurt…terribly. I wanted this finished for her. Maria bore down again and the child had passed into life and into the bright lights of the world of television. She heard his first cries. Her baby was born.

I had done what I said I would do. I created an egg with the DNA of Jesus. Maria made the rest of it possible. We had done it. But we failed to ask the most prudent of questions: should we have done it?

I stared around at the others who were so honored to be there to witness the birth of the new Messiah. In a small crowd tucked behind the director, a face stood out. The face struck me as a mixture of youthfulness and hardened experience. The two looks were odd together. Out of every person on the set he seemed to be the oddest one here.

I must have stared a little too long. His eyes caught mine and suddenly he dropped back and out of sight. I pressed through the crowd to get a better look, but my movements were too slow. By the time I reached the other side of the crowd, he was gone. Who was he? Thirty years later I would see his face once again, but at that time he was only an odd face at an odd time.

Then the dust will return to the earth as it was, And the soul will return to God who gave it. — *Ecclesiastes 12:7*

CHAPTER 7

Father Russo visited me one windy, cool autumn day just as the sun fell beneath the buildings near my office. He had read a verse in the Bible that troubled him. It was a new verse to me. I had never seen it before, but then again, I wasn't much of a Bible reader. I left that to guys like Russo and Thompson.

"This disturbs me, Matthew," the priest said. "Isaiah 53:2 says, 'He grew up before him like a tender shoot, and like a root out of dry ground. He had no beauty or majesty to attract us to him, nothing in his appearance that we should desire him.'"

When Jesus walked the earth two thousand years ago, very little was recorded about his tender childhood and teen years. He was found in a temple and he traveled to Egypt. There was speculation that he journeyed to the Far East, but it was just speculation, at best. Isaiah's prophecy gave little else. He grew up like a tender root. Jesus wasn't a handsome young man. He wouldn't have made it in Hollywood.

How different from his Twentieth Century clone. During his growing years, I visited monthly to observe and check his body. We wanted to make sure that there were no problems with the cloned material. His days were filled with Bible study and Bible memorization. He was raised to know all the scriptures by heart. His personal trainer made sure that his body could endure the stress of living the pace of being the Messiah.

The fact that "he had no beauty or majesty to attract us" bothered Russo and Thompson. "This could be damaging to television ratings," Russo said. The medium was increasingly the way to spread the message, but he had to have a TV presence. Image had become everything. They couldn't see anything that they recognized as "knock 'em dead" good looks. In that meeting, he had asked me to find a plastic surgeon. I told them it wasn't necessary. No matter what he looked like, he was a media figure. Russo left as quickly as he had come. I didn't think my words gave him any comfort, but in time they discovered I was right.

My monthly visits were brief and primarily for scientific reasons. As I sat with him in each visit, something bothered me, but I was never quite sure what it was. All the correct physical functions were resident, but I was convinced that there was something missing in his humanity. But I could have been wrong. I tried to convince myself that it was his godhood. Believe me, I had nothing to compare it to, so I was left wondering.

I struggled often with the question of exactly what it was. Beth and I sat up many nights. She thought that I wrestled with the question of whether or not I should have done the cloning. I admit I often felt like I was living out the life of Mary Shelley's Dr. Frankenstein. I was so obsessed with the doing of the project that I never stopped to ask the whys. It seemed like I was locked inside a bad black and white horror movie.

I struggled on that level, but there was never any real reason to doubt Jesus's goodness. He was very mechanical in his approach. At times he seemed very wooden in his actions and reactions. As a boy, he would quote a verse and walk away. As a young man, he began rearranging the verses to make them his own words. If the Jesus of the Bible walked the earth in our time, he would have spoken like the clone.

There was little to worry about concerning his media appeal. If I walked into a grocery store in any city of the world, a tabloid flashed his picture with a sensational headline. "Jesus Healed My Cancer When I Walked By His Picture." That was a good one, but my favorite was "Jesus and Elvis Together." The rag even had photos of the two eating dinner at Graceland. No, there was no worry about his media appeal.

The Prophet Thompson would feature Jesus on his show at least once a month. America, Europe, and the rest of the world saw their new savior grow up before their eyes. I felt as if I was watching little Opie grow into Richie, and then into Ron Howard, and finally into the mega talented director. Now I was watching Jesus, only he was directing the world and all the people on it. Truly, to him all the world was a stage.

Every time I saw him, that same question gnawed at me. What was it that was missing? When he had reached his thirtieth birthday, Beth and I attended a party in his honor on a cool, crisp Christmas Eve. He had developed quite a commanding presence in a room. His mind was sharp, his body was toned, and the world hung on his every word. Maria was also there. Her comments finally put all my questions into a neat package.

"Doctor, could we speak alone for a few minutes?" she asked.

Beth excused herself to get some more punch and to talk to Laura, Prophet Thompson's personal assistant. Maria and I slipped out to the lawn in front of the mansion where Jesus was raised. The house had been donated by a supporter and follower, and was in Central Italy and far from reporters and intruders.

"What is it, Maria? I don't think I've ever seen you as distressed as this. Is there something wrong with Jesus?" I quizzed.

"Yes, I think so," she answered in her Italian accent. Maria's eyes filled with tears and she began to sob.

While my heart beat hard in my chest, I put my hands on both of her shoulders. "What is it?" Her tears and emotion let me know it was truly serious, but I needed to have answers to my question. "Maria, it will be okay. Just tell me what the problem is and I can take care of it."

"Not this one, Doctor. You cannot give him what I think is missing," she spoke.

"What's missing? What do you mean?" I asked, as if I didn't have my own doubts and fears that something was missing. I needed to know what she saw and felt.

"Jesus is a man, but he's not the God-man." She started to weep again. Her breast rose and fell in deep sobs. I pulled her out of the view of the mansion toward the maze of bushes in the yard.

"Maria, I know what you mean. Beth and I have felt for a long time that there is something missing in our cloned version of the Messiah. Why do you say that he isn't the God-man?" I probed, but also wanted to reassure her that I understood what she was talking about.

"The Bible is very plain that my spirit should bear witness to the fact that this is the true Messiah. I do not sense that he has a spiritual nature. He has no soul." Maria seemed puzzled as she spoke.

I wasn't a theologian, and Maria wasn't a Bible student either. The possibility that she could be wrong was too high. We talked about it further in the months that followed, but always in the greatest secrecy. At what point did the soul enter the human body? I couldn't answer that question. Thoughts and questions were racing through my head, but I knew I had to answer Maria with some direction.

"Maria, this is something very hard to prove or even comprehend. I don't think you should say any of this to another person. I'm not sure what they would do if they knew how you felt," I told her, and we went back into the party.

Carefully chosen media people were covering the event. I put the *Time, Newsweek,* and *Life* magazines with Jesus on the cover in my files. He was thirty and primed to begin his ministry.

Sometimes it was hard for me to believe that I had been physically present at the key events of my generation...in fact, of the century. I was wandering around when one large man from a South American country stepped back and collided with me. Much like one of those chain reaction car wrecks, I tipped off balance to my side and struck a man holding a drink in his hand. The contents were tossed from the glass onto the man's suit jacket.

"I'm so sorry," I told him, while reaching into my pocket for my handkerchief.

"That's all right, Dr. MacDonald," he said. I looked up at this face, and recognized it immediately. Although it had been thirty years since I saw it last on the night that Jesus was born, I recognized it. It was his face. The youthfulness had been replaced by middle age, but the hardness was still there. The thirty years had carved the tension of life into every crease and crevice of his features.

I started to say something when a loud speaker drew my attention away from him for a second. I looked back and he was gone. The fellow he had been talking to was still in the same spot.

"Excuse me, but I noticed that you were talking to a man a few minutes ago. I was sure that I knew him but can't remember his name. That's so embarrassing in social situations like this. Refresh my memory so I can talk to him later," I told him.

"That was Jack Hesidence."

"Oh, yes, yes. Now I remember," I said, as I acted like the name belonged to an old friend. "I haven't seen him for years. I wonder what his connection to the Messiah is?"

"He's a delegate from his country," the man told me.

"What country?"

"The United States, of course," he exclaimed in amazement that I didn't know. "You just bumped into the Director of the C.I.A. You better be careful next time." I was puzzled and it must have shown on my face, because the man spoke to me again. "I meant that as a joke." I laughed and pardoned myself.

All these are the beginning of sorrows. Then they will deliver you up to tribulation and kill you, and you will be hated by all nations for My name's sake.
— *Matthew 24:8-9*

CHAPTER 8

A few hundred miles south of the mansion, a lonely and troubled man sat in what is known as the Chair of Peter. For over thirty years Father Russo had craftily manipulated the Vatican. He had gained great support for his cloned Messiah among the other members of the Catholic clergy. It was hard to stop Russo's climb to monsignor, and then bishop. Stopping the young bishop would have been more like stopping a runaway train. The pope sat, according to his memoirs, agonizing over the events that continued to unfold in front of him. These were events that he could not control and could not quash even in their earliest stages. He felt powerless against a force that he was unable to identify.

The pope had held the clone at a distance. He was always afraid to embrace him or to meet with him, because it would give credence and support to Jesus's ministry. He wasn't about to do that. With a quill pen and an inkwell he scratched this prayer across paper.

My Lord, I do not understand Your ways and yet I seek them. I have come to You begging on my knees, on my face, in fasting, in repentance, and yet no answer has come. I have felt no peace about this man who bears the name and genetics of Your true Son.

I have no peace about his deity. I have no peace about his purpose. I have no peace about his companions. Even scripture says in Mark's gospel, "And if any man shall say to you, Lo, here is Christ; or, lo, he is there; believe him not.' If he is the Messiah, reveal this to me. Do not let me or the world be deceived. I cry unto You. I beg.

I still do not understand Your ways. They are higher than mine. In all of this I feel no peace, but I know that You control every aspect, every twist, and the final outcome. I submit my will to Yours.

On the same night that Maria confessed her confusion, the Holy Father wrote his prayer of confession and confusion. It was on the same night that Jesus started his ministry from a celebrity laden party that filled a mansion designed for monarchs. There was no John the Baptist. There was no baptism with a descending dove, and no pronouncement of him being God's son by a heavenly voice. There was no declaration that he was the lamb of God. No one ate locust or honey. Instead, champagne and martinis flowed and tiny sandwiches were fed into mouths.

I walked back inside through the garden doors and into the large dining area. Bishop Russo was standing on a chair to get the attention of the crowd. I looked around me at a sea of dignitaries, movie stars, world leaders, and economic powers. They had come to meet, to be with, to celebrate with, Jesus of Nazareth. How strange that the same type of powers that had crucified the body of Jesus more than two thousand years before stood at attention waiting for his entrance and blessing. If there had been palm fronds, I think they would have cast them down for Jesus to walk on.

"Ladies and gentlemen, for thirty years, my friend Tom...excuse me, you know him as the Prophet Thompson...and I have celebrated birthdays with our Lord Jesus. Tom and I laughed that only twenty-eight years ago, we had a group of clowns here to entertain him. Today, this room is filled with the world's greatest politicians."

A voice heckled from the crowd, "It hasn't changed much, has it?"

Russo smiled. The comment was funny but inappropriate. They had come to celebrate the birthday of the Prince of Peace. "I'm sorry for that interruption. Tonight, we are going to do more than celebrate his thirty years of life. Tonight, Jesus is announcing his entrance into public ministry."

***

Thompson and Russo never missed a chance for media coverage. The major cable news networks beamed Russo's comments and Christ's announcement around the world, but not everyone considered Jesus the darling of their parties.

In the United States, a group of conservative pastors had voiced their concerns in writing, in their churches, and in media settings. The Protestant church was dividing over following the Messiah clone or rejecting him. The new Prince of Peace didn't bring peace to the churches. Then again, I would have suspected that. They had such little unity to begin with. Most people blamed it on the fringe radical right.

It was the words of *Christianity Today* editor, Ken Sidee, that struck the hardest but had the greatest wisdom. He wrote in one of his editorials, "We are confronted with a new faith. For the first time, evangelicals—who have said that faith is believing in the unseen, not the seen—must deal with a Jesus that can be seen. We are left with two camps...those who say, 'To deny him is to be a Pharisee.' And those who preach out, 'To accept him is to be a fool.' As yet, we have seen no sign that he is genuine, but we have seen no sign that he is a charlatan either. As Jesus launches into his public ministry, we may see the truth. I believe rather than the truth setting us free, it will polarize us even further. I pray my prophecy does not come true."

The conservative camps grew stronger over the thirty years, yet with time even those divided and split. One group wanted to prepare for the coming "tribulation" spoken of in the Book of Revelation. They gave up their homes and stopped using any traceable form of money or credit. Some groups moved into secret dwellings in the mountains.

I wasn't aware of the battles that raged. In Zurich, Beth and I were quite comfortable. Only major news stories filtered into our home. Evangelical battles didn't seem major to the media in Switzerland. Russo and Thompson never mentioned them either. It wasn't until I began my research into the truth behind the Messiah clone that I discovered the other factors.

***

I wandered through the crowd at the birthday party until Beth caught me from behind. She was still with Laura.

"How does Laura stay with that bag of wind Thompson?" I whispered into my wife's ear next to her teardrop black pearl Tahitian earring. Then I turned my attention to our old friend. "Hello, Laura. It is really good to see you again."

"Matthew, this is quite a night, isn't it? I can't believe the people who are here," she rattled off as she shot her eyes from side to side. She was afraid to miss any one of the famous guests. "Tom would like you and Beth to come to breakfast tomorrow morning. The bishop and Jesus will be joining us as well. Can you make it?"

Beth butted in, "I told her it was okay. We aren't leaving till the afternoon, I believe."

"Sure, Laura, it would be wonderful just to sit and talk with you. Have you talked to Maria tonight?" I asked.

"She seemed troubled about something. I think it's hard for her to see her little boy grow up," Laura answered.

What a stupid answer. Jesus was never her little boy. She was the vehicle for his birth. Russo had her stay around more like a wet nurse than a mother. The bishop was mother, father, and teacher to Jesus. I was glad to hear that Laura had no idea what was bothering Maria. I would have feared for Maria had she been talking further beyond me. I didn't know why, but I would have.

I heard applause and turned my head. Jesus had entered the room. It wasn't quite palm branches, but the clapping would have to do. The monthly visits had been suspended a few years back, so it had been several months since I last saw him, and I was surprised. Jesus had let his hair grow out. It was a dark brown with a wave to it. His brown eyes were piercing, as if they looked into your soul. He wasn't quite six foot tall, but the build of his body was solid. The personal trainer's strict health and fitness routine was bearing strong fruit. As I entered I noticed he had, not surprisingly, started a beard. It wasn't yet filled in, as spots of skin peaked through.

He raised his hands and everyone cheered. There was a euphoria in the room. I forgot even my own deep questions...I forgot Maria's questioning. I was lifted with the moment. He dropped his hands and the room's decibel level dropped. Even the sound of an ice cube clinking against a glass was overpowering. There was absolute silence. I thought back to the story of Jesus calming the storm. He told the sea to "shut up," and the waters obeyed and became placid. In the same way this modern day Messiah commanded us to silence with a mere dropping of his hands. The crowd became placid.

"Blessed are the peacemakers. In my first incarnation, I spoke those words. But peace did not come. Instead, the religious leaders of that age, the Jews, who will despise you, rejected my peaceful presence. They took my body and they nailed it to a cross. No peace was had. The world continued to wage war as it does even today. I have come again. This time, I have come to bring peace to the world."

Applause rose as if timed for the cameras. It thundered. My head was hurting from the sound. It was also hurting from trying to understand what was going on around me. Russo's face glowed like an attending angel slapping his hands together as if they were cherub's wings. He was flying tonight. Jesus raised his hands and the audience hushed.

"In my daily time of prayer, the Father has led me to this day to make my announcement concerning my entrance into the ministry. In my first incarnation, I stood in the temple and read from the book of Isaiah. That announcement brought me ridicule and a near stoning, as it would most likely bring today. I do hope tonight my words fall on more receptive ears," he said with a well-placed smile that reflected his well-placed tongue-in-cheek remark.

"Yes, yes," the crowd screamed back. They erupted again into clapping, only this time the words "yes" and "amen" joined the swelling noises. I felt like I was trapped in the sea. The gentle swaying of the crowd made me nauseous, but I didn't want to leave.

I looked again at my handiwork. Jesus had grown strong, with sharp Middle-eastern features. He looked Jewish. He looked the way I had always imagined the Messiah had looked. Here before me was the body and blood of Jesus...but was the soul of Jesus there?

"Let me finish, I will begin my mission tomorrow. I depart for the United States soon with my good friend and co-worker, The Prophet Reverend Thomas Thompson. From that point I will appear wherever the spirit leads me. For I have come to bring a peace that passes all understanding to this world." He ended his speech and stepped down off the platform that had been erected for his use.

He passed through the crowd. World leaders greeted him, hugged him, and promised their support. Jesus smiled. I watched him move so freely about people. He had something unique when it came to personalities. He read each person quickly and adjusted to be what they needed. I wouldn't say it was chameleon-like...the shift happened more out of an intuitive response than from a desire to be loved. He had all the adoration he needed.

He brushed passed me, and his dark eyes shot a glance towards me. Did he know what I was thinking?

"Matthew, I am so glad you're here. Why didn't you and Beth come upstairs when you got here? Don't tell me Russo has you believing that he has me on a short leash? I've missed our times together. My travels will be quite extensive so I won't be around much, but I'll have the prophet fly you to meet us on a regular basis. We'll try to make it someplace warm so you can get that beautiful wife of yours out of dreary Zurich this time of the year." He hugged me and turned to go on, but as he took his first step, he moved his head towards me and said, "My spirit tells me that your spirit is very heavy. I'll make sure I pray for you this evening."

As he turned away a shifting shadow passed over him and hovered like a cloud. It was odd that in a room filled with lights from every direction that a solitary shadow would move so freely without being refracted. Jesus's words and that shadow conflicted my soul deeply. Something churned and soured in my stomach, and I raced for the marble balcony off the back of the mansion. I needed air. I needed pure, fresh air.

For when they say, "Peace and safety!" then sudden destruction comes upon them, as labor pains upon a pregnant woman. And they shall not escape.
— I Thessalonians 5:3

CHAPTER 9

He began his ministry one week and one day after the day of his Christmas Eve announcement. I sometimes wondered if the event was set up by Russo and Thompson. My knowledge of time and place came only from watching it on TV and reading about it months later.

New Years Day was more than the beginning of a new year. This was the first year that the street gangs of the United States were gathering for a conference. Chicago was the city of choice, for natural reasons. I found it fairly hard to understand how a group of street thugs, murderers, drug dealers, and various other criminals could so openly hold a conference. Political parties had conferences, doctors had conferences, and even carpet cleaners had conferences, but gangs? Their purpose was simple: unify all gangs for financial and bodily security.

The urban streets had a reddish stain in many of our major cities. The blacks attacked the Hispanics and the Hispanics attacked the Vietnamese, and they in turn hit other oriental gangs. It was bloody. Many lives had been lost, so they called for a conference.

Somehow, I didn't picture this conference with red hats and drunken old men chasing young women of questionable character. The scenes on TV verified my guesses. Every door to the large conference room was protected by guards in black hats, black leather jackets, and large black Uzis. No one got in except those they wanted in.

The first day's activities were filled with speeches from African American, Hispanic American, Vietnamese American, and Caucasian social leaders. Major political figures addressed these young men and women. They called for disarmament and peace for the cities.

The speeches were eloquent but pandering, filled with phrases like, "You are the future of this country," and "You are the leaders of tomorrow." They sounded more like commencement addresses. In a way, maybe this was a commencement, or some type of beginning. We were going to legitimize the pain and suffering the gangs had brought to our streets. With that, our nation would legalize their operations. It angered me as I watched. I probably should have turned it off, but like all voyeurs of society's decline, I sat in couch potato position absorbing the broadcast reality.

By evening, the gangs had called for some sort of unification. After another hour of seesaw yelling speckled with fist fights, the conventioneers decided to select a leader who would speak and act for them.

The lead figure was D-Boy Patterson. I snickered when the newsman covering the story moved into a split screen set-up and gave a review of Patterson's "career." I thought I was watching a political rally, except the crimes listed on Patterson's sheet weren't as white collar as those we would see on a politician's rap sheet. Many thought Patterson's name of D-Boy was short for Devon, his given first name. But it was for Dead Boy, because he had killed more people dead before he reached the age of thirteen than any other member of his gang. The bodies that dropped around him after the age of thirteen ranged beyond the color commentator's resource information. In other words, D-Boy was a killer. He enjoyed it. It made him money and it gave him power.

In an interview, D-Boy talked about killing. He felt as if he took the power from the person he killed and added it to his own, and he wanted all the power he could get. D-Boy was feared, but he was also followed.

He had become a folk hero to young inner city kids who had no fathers to look up to and mothers who had neglected them for the crack houses. When D-Boy hit the streets, his car was the finest, his clothes were the best, and his women were the most beautiful. He had it all in the eyes of a poor kid who barely ate once a day. He had fulfilled the American Dream, or rather the American Nightmare.

The opposition in the gang leader election was only known as Mo. It stood for mo' money, mo' cars, mo' drugs, mo' fun, mo'.... Mo was older than D-Boy, and after years of negotiation with other gangs, he had brought New York City a modicum of peace. Mo really was a community organizer, only he did it with a gun. He was a very dangerous leader that usually got what he wanted, or the opposition got what they least wanted.

D-Boy and Mo stood on the stage of the convention hall. D-Boy had only one thing in mind: taking Mo's power in the only way he knew. He knew that if he lost,

Mo was to be assassinated within one minute. D-Boy would get what he wanted.

This was no ordinary convention to begin with, but it was the next event that brought it from a news story to be a significant point of reference in history.

D-Boy was elected president, or leader. I don't remember which it was. Mo congratulated him; we all knew the battle between the two would rage on, but the scene was good for a photo op. The cable news stations would love that one. The past careers of Mo and D-Boy would be chalked up to the evils of a Eurocentric government and economic system by the more radical leaning commentators. One suspiciously ordained commentator had already tweeted that D-Boy was a new black Messiah. They would be written up like they were the present day Jesse James and Billy the Kid. No, they would make the two killers more like Robin Hood.

D-Boy began his address to the gathered gangs. He was aware that the last address of the night was coming from Jesus himself. In the interview he had admitted that he accepted the plan to bring Jesus into the center of it all because of what he represented. To D-Boy, Jesus was a symbol of the white man's religion. D-Boy had his own version of faith. It was the two pistols he carried at all times. In those, he could find faith to make it every day, and deliver unholy judgment on anyone who sinned against him.

To D-Boy, Jesus was also the most powerful man in the world. To have Jesus's power would mean he was unstoppable as the leader of the nation's gangs. He coveted what that would lead to. His plan was simple. As Jesus held up his hands to address the gangs, D-Boy would simply slip a barrel of one of his guns into Jesus's side and shoot. Nothing clean about it, but the job would be done. He would be powerful, he would be feared, and he would be untouchable. D-Boy would be their god after Jesus was dead. Sure, he would go into hiding, protected by gangs in every city of the country.

Jesus was flanked by Russo and two men. Later, their names and faces became very familiar to me. At that time, I only saw them as bodyguards. He touched hands, accepted worship, and moved deliberately down the center aisle to the platform. D-Boy waited. His way to power didn't have to occur at that moment. It could wait a few minutes. The TV camera's revealed an intensity in D-Boy's eyes. I could tell from the close-up shots that something big was going to happen. Something very big. I was surprised that Russo would put Jesus into such a position.

Jesus took a few more steps and was stopped by a young woman who fell at his feet, kissing them. She was weeping, her chest heaving with torrents of emotion as Jesus reached down and pulled the woman to her feet. She stared at him and he spoke to her. I thought I could make out the words, "Your sins are forgiven." It bugged me. If I wasn't absolutely sure he was the Messiah, then how could he be so undeniably sure? He was touching her face with both hands when he said it. Jesus released her face and walked towards the platform. It was like he knew where he was going and what he was going to do there.

Jesus did know. His steps were deliberate and strong to the bottom of the stairs leading to the platform, where he looked up. No smile was on his face, but no smile received him either. The clone set his jaw and walked up the stairs. I could see D-Boy fidgeting with something under his jacket.

Jesus was on the platform. He rotated his head and looked into the camera. It was there that he smiled, but it was the eyes that kept giving him away. People talk about the eyes being the window to the soul. What happens when you don't have a soul? The eyes become a window to what?

He stepped across the stage to the podium. D-Boy stood blocking his path and they stood, face-to-face, eye-to-eye. I wish the camera angle had allowed me to see Jesus's eyes, or even D-Boy's. The gang leader moved for something under his coat. His arm tensed, along with the entire crowd of conventioneers.

Thousands of miles away in my Switzerland home, my stomach knotted. I couldn't believe that Russo had put Jesus in harm's way. It didn't seem like a thing Russo would do. He had done it though, and I had to watch it.

Suddenly, a shadow raced across the stage. Maybe it was the camera or the lights, I thought, but it appeared to be a shadow of a human being. It dropped its blackness on each person on stage, and they stopped and dropped back like confusion had come over them. Some rubbed their eyes. One guy shook his head like he was tossing off a shroud. Then the shadow stopped. I wondered if I was the only one seeing it.

The shadow crept almost imperceptibly towards the two characters in their deadlocked stare down. D-Boy was still fumbling under his coat, and everything inside told me he was going for a gun. I tensed my muscles and clenched my teeth so hard that pain shot to my brain. I had to know what D-Boy had, and what was causing the shadow?

The shadow inched closer to D-Boy, and his head jerked once. The shadow engulfed the gangsta's head and

D-Boy stumbled, losing his balance for a second and falling out of the shadow.

D-Boy's head snapped in Jesus's direction. His mouth twisted to a sneer just before the shadow made a broad leap across the stage, covering the young man totally. D-Boy stiffened and his face quickly contorted. Then it relaxed and a new smile came over his face.

D-Boy's arm relaxed, and he let go of the bulge in his coat. His head dropped, breaking the intense eye to eye glare at Jesus. His tall body slumped. Something broke within him. Something snapped. D-Boy turned to the podium and set his face towards the microphone, but it wasn't his face at all. The features were the same, but the muscles moved differently across the bones.

"Brothers and sisters, we gathered here to bring unity and to end the wars between our gangs. I was elected your leader. Today, I call for us to lay down our arms and come together to work for the restoration of the cities we have destroyed. I call for us to reaffirm our spiritual heritage and fall before the new Messiah." D-Boy's voice was clear but there was a quivering, a shaking deep inside him.

Jesus turned and walked down the steps and towards the door. The world had witnessed the most powerful display of peacemaking in history, but had anyone else seen the shadow? It all looked like peace, but I was beginning to believe that there was more behind it.

Jesus strolled out the door. The bodyguards kept reporters away. He then slipped into his car and they were gone.

D-Boy moved away from the podium. The conference was over, and the conventioneers cleared the room. The floor was covered with guns and the remnants of gang colors. I was shocked as I watched. The reporters were stunned. It was more like a work of fiction than reality. Actually, it was more like science fiction.

What had happened? That was the big question. Actually, that seemed to be the only question. It wasn't until months later that D-Boy surfaced again to give an interview. Not much had been heard from or about him. He had faded from the scene like a bad character in a sitcom. It was all clear to me when he said, "I looked into that Jesus's eyes. We stared for a long time...it felt like eternity — my eternity. I saw deep in his eyes, the blackness, the emptiness, and the lostness of Hell. If Hell was what I saw in those eyes, then I didn't want to go there. Then something grabbed my brain inside my skull. I couldn't breathe, went dizzy, and stumbled. Moments later I recovered, only to be gripped again. That time it was my whole body, mind, and — yeah, even I'll have to say it — my spirit. If this is Jesus, then as my grandmother used to say, 'Jesus is God.' If this is God, then I see a bitter hate inside him. That hate was directly focused on me. I don't think I had much choice when I stood face to face and eye to eye on that platform. I don't even remember making the speech asking for the gangs to put down their weapons and follow Jesus. Even when I watch the video of it, I see someone else standing there with my clothes on, and using my face and my mouth to speak to the world. I saw the most intense look of hate and the reality of what God's hate would do to me. I changed. I had to."

This was the most revealing account of what had happened. My eyes saw something that my brain didn't understand. The information was collected and I logged it into my memory.

And you will hear of wars and rumors of wars. See that you are not troubled; for all these things must come to pass, but the end is not yet. For nation will rise against nation, and kingdom against kingdom. And there will be famines, pestilences, and earthquakes in various places.
— Matthew 24:26

CHAPTER 10

The following months were filled with event after event. Headlines read, "Jesus Heals" or "Jesus Brings Peace" or "Jesus Meets World Leaders." These were all things that had been in the news. Nothing I need to remind anyone of, but there was one thing that bothered me through the events. If Jesus was the Messiah, then his kingdom was supposed to be a religious one. Over those fast paced months, the clone met with many heads of state to discuss the world economic situation and social crises. As his world tour ended, a group of nations formulated a loose bond.

The bond tightened as time went on. The charter members numbered ten at first. Three member nations — Spain, Portugal, and France — were tenuous as Jesus, his prophet, and Bishop Russo applied pressure for a tighter coalition. The tensions in Eastern Europe were threatening to rip apart other unions of nations. The Middle East seethed as it had. The new coalition would have a special power, one greater than the rest. It would be the power of the Messiah.

Their unifying bond would be him. I read about miracles and prophecies done before these world leaders to convince them to join. He materialized food. He even walked on water. I tried to figure out how he could have done it. What was the trick? Or was it the real thing? If it was real, then where did the power come from?

Out of the original ten, the three were uncomfortable and chose to withdraw. It was a mistake. Massive movements of armed vehicles and soldiers pressed in from all areas. Navies stood off the shores, ready to fire on command. The American prophet predicted famine and pestilence over the three dissenting nations. And like all his prophecies, the famine followed a week in which the nations' crops were bizarrely attacked by a fog of locusts. With the military presence around them and their crops eaten by hordes of locusts, the three crumbled. It was inevitable. The withering citizens of the three dissenters cried out for "peace and prosperity" to fall upon their once productive and rich lands. The presidents and leaders of the three eventually surrendered control to the Messiah and to his rule. The ten nations rose up in Europe like some kind of dragon from the sea.

I had never thought, when I was sitting in my lab trying to formulate the egg, that this would be the result. I remembered a conversation with Beth after one of my incredibly long weekends of trial and error. We were lying in bed, my red eyes had already rolled back in my head, and the lids had closed tight for the night. She startled me from my badly needed rest with a finger poke in the rib.

"Hey, are you asleep?"

"I was, but not anymore," I groaned.

She rolled towards me and propped her head on her upstretched forearm and hand. Even through bleary and sleepy eyes, she looked great. "I was wondering, when you finally create your little Jesus egg and he grows up, what do you think he'll do?"

I may have surprised her that I was so quick and lucid with an answer following just waking up. "You know, I've been thinking about that as I worked. I see him as able to answer some of the great religious questions that we all have. Like, why are there so many religions? And why do children have to suffer? And the most important, why do wives wake their husbands up to ask silly questions?"

"It wasn't silly. I've been thinking about it. It's actually troubled me a lot. How do we know that he won't turn out bad?"

She had asked a good question. It was one I really hadn't thought about, and I admitted this. "Don't know, but if he's Jesus he'll be good. He could turn out to be the savior of the world. I think most people will look to him for religious answers. They'll be curious to see what Jesus looked and talked like. I'm not sure that Russo or Thompson have thought it out either. Which surprises me, because Father Russo figures out every possible angle before he makes a step."

"Then he's probably thought about that scenario as well. Do you realize that the clone could turn out to be wicked?"

"Impossible, Beth. This is Jesus we're talking about here," I snapped back, out of defense for my project.

"Matthew, you are only cloning a body. Just tissue."

What she said had struck a strong blow to my reality. There wasn't any guarantee for what I was doing; none at all. I rolled over and pretended to sleep. I couldn't though; Beth's question had given me the thin edge of a doubt.

I don't think that this particular scenario of Jesus as a world political and religious leader had ever crossed my mind. Not even that evening when I laid awake wondering. His power had grown far beyond what I imagined it would be. Jesus's kingdom wasn't of this earth, but the clone's kingdom had grown large and powerful on this globe.

He still had a few obstacles left. One of them sat in Rome in Peter's chair. The ten kingdoms were linked by their religion, but the head of that link wasn't that sure of the veracity of the clone. The pope refused to allow the church to enter into this bond with the ten nations. This was a grave mistake on his part.

Thus he said: The fourth beast shall be A fourth kingdom on earth, which shall be different from all other kingdoms, and shall devour the whole earth, trample it and break it in pieces. The ten horns are ten kings who shall arise from this kingdom. And another shall rise after them; He shall be different from the first ones, and shall subdue three kings. — Daniel 7:23-24

CHAPTER 11

The diary Bishop Russo accidentally left behind in my lab has proven to be extremely informative. I've gained more insight into the twisted and deviant plans of Russo than I ever wanted to learn. He was meticulous in expressing his feelings in words and drafting out his step-by-step plan. On the day that Bishop Russo barged into my laboratory, it was different. Something in the clone was beginning to trouble him.

"Matthew, I'm sorry to disturb you. I didn't call before I flew up here because I wanted no one to know where I was going. We've got to talk. I need some answers right away." Russo seemed desperate. Over the years I had grown to mistrust this beady-eyed man. This was a new side of him...a weaker, uncontrolled side that actually appealed to me.

"Bishop Russo, I don't think I've ever seen you like this before. What's got a burr under your saddle?" I questioned.

"It's that damned clone of yours," the bishop responded.

"My clone now. I feel like a father when the son does something wrong. All of a sudden the mother cries out, 'That son of yours.' So, what did my son do now?"

"I'm sure you've been watching the news. You know about his peacemaking trips around the world. These things have changed him. At one time, I felt as if he was working with the Prophet Thompson and me. Now, it's like we are working for him. There has been a radical change in his personality. Could it be some kind of genetic problem?" he asked.

"Maybe; I don't know. I could run some tests on him to see if there is a problem. Personally, I think that he's starting to believe his own press," I said as I folded up my books. I placed them on the shelf next to my desk as I tried to place the blame a little closer to home for Russo.

"If he is, then that cloned Messiah is going to foul up the plans we've set." He grimaced, plowing deep hard lines across his face.

"Are they your plans? Or are they his plans? Have you stopped to question whether or not they are God's plans? I think it's time that you and the mighty prophet start to examine your motivations in this project," I snapped out self-righteously.

"Like your motivation was so high and lofty. The moment I mentioned a million dollars you were on board. So, don't give me that holier than thou crap. You're just like Thompson and me," he lashed back at me. His words stung because they were true. I had examined my motivation, and what I did was more for me than anyone else involved. I felt convicted and deserved his comment.

"I'm sorry, John. You're right. He scares me. His leadership of this ten nation European Union has established him as a world power broker; and the possibility of joining those ten nations to the mother church frightens me even more," I confided.

"Don't be too worried about that. His Eminence, the Pope, is racing to pull away from the linking of the Union and the church. I've tried to convince him that world peace could be achieved by placing such a moral rudder at the headship of new European Union, but he isn't buying it," Russo explained. He sat back in the big leather chair opposite my desk and rubbed his face hard with his two hands, like he was trying to bring the blood to his brain so he could think clearly.

"Look, John...why don't you fly back to Rome, grab our clone, and bring him in for a hundred thousand mile check-up? If there is something I can do, then we'll do it. Like I said, though, I think he's simply believing all that's been told to him," I said in as calming of a voice as possible, while inside I started to unravel.

Russo snapped to his feet. His nervousness had apparently not left him. When he reached down and snatched up his battered, leather brief case, his quick movement tipped it and the contents went sprawling across my lab floor. I bent down to help him and he glanced up at me. His eyes had a sadness in them that allowed me to see his heart. "I guess I wanted a Jesus with flesh on him, and now I'm trying to control him. I'm wrong in that, aren't I?"

"I don't know, John. I really don't know," I answered as I shook my head.

The bishop was probably on his flight back to Rome by the time I sat at my desk again. As I swung my feet under it, my shoe kicked something. The item slid out of the other side of the desk. I got up and went around to see what it was, and found a thick, leather-bound book. At first I thought it was Russo's Bible. I put it on my desk, thinking that I'd post it down to him in Rome the next day. If it hadn't been for Beth's phone call, I would have done just that without even opening the book.

"Matthew," her voice came through the phone. I loved to hear her voice. "I heard something on TV today that troubled me. It was a Biblical reference. So, I guess I've got a Bible question for you."

"What luck. Bishop Russo was just in and he accidentally dropped his Bible. I've got it right here on my desk, so spit it out," I responded playfully.

"What was that son of a – ?"

"Now, Beth," I shot out to stop her. Beth had never liked the bishop, and I was sure with good reason. "He had some concerns about Jesus and he needed to ask me some questions. Anyway, he's gone. So, ask me the question?"

"The guy on TV said that in the last days before Christ returns, there would the formation of ten nations into a union under a religious leader. Where is that in the Bible?" she questioned.

"I'm not sure, but probably in that last book, Revelations," I answered. "Let me see."

I picked up the heavy, thick, black leather volume and turned to the back section. It was blank. I flipped forward until I found pages covered not in Bible verses, but in the handwritten scrawl of John Russo. His diary entries went back to before we met. It wasn't a daily record, but from its appearance, it was an important record of the major events in the clone's life.

"Beth, I'll have to call you back on that. Something just came up. Something very important." I hung up the phone and rushed down the hall to the copier room. My heart was thumping. What if Russo discovered it missing and was heading back to get it? I needed his notes so I could know his thoughts. I had to copy this and get it back to him before he became suspicious. I flipped through page after page, copying for the next two hours. My eyes, feet, and back were sore, but I needed to get these notes to a safe place where I could read them.

As I was lost in thought over my current project, I heard fast paced steps clicking down the hall. My office was the only room on that narrow hallway of the building. The steps had the cadence of a man in a great hurry. I grabbed my notes and the diary, flipped off the light, and slid behind the door to the copier room. There was only one way out and one way in.

My heart beat so loudly in my mouth that I was sure it alone was enough to betray my hiding place. The footsteps hurried by the door and further on. Then I heard my office door handle jiggle. Whoever it was, they wanted to see me.

The clicking steps reversed and headed back down the hall towards me. I wanted to run. I wanted to hide. I wanted to be invisible. The steps clicked to a sudden stop outside the door. The light from the hall cut a white, four foot long rectangle on the copier room floor. The person in the hallway stepped towards the half open door. His shadow started into the rectangle, moving like the rising bands of heat racing up from the ground on a hot August day. The shadow suddenly stopped and moved no further. I listened for the sound of my visitor's breathing. Nothing. It was dead quiet.

The hand of the shadowy figure raised from its side until the tip of the shadow touched the copier. Suddenly the whirring sound of the machine fan stopped and the lights on the control board went dead. The shadow receded and then slowed as it retreated. I waited for it to wrap around the door and grasp me. Then suddenly the clicking heels headed off down the hall.

I waited a few minutes before I moved back to the machine and tried the on switch. Nothing happened. I clicked it on and off several times, but nothing happened. How could a shadow shut off a machine and render it inoperative? The whole affair was starting to frighten me, and there were two more pages to copy. I needed those copies.

I walked into my office and saw my flatbed scanner. I booted up my computer system and decided to finish off the copying that way. It took me a few moments, and then I wrapped the diary to send it back. I had to cover my tracks and make Russo believe that I never saw the inside of the diary.

I scribbled a note to him. "Dear John, Your Bible fell out of your briefcase when you were here. I didn't think a bishop should be without the main tool of his trade. I'm sending it off to you within minutes of your departure. Who knows, with the slowness of air travel and the lateness of flights, it may beat you back to Rome." I hoped the humor would disarm any suspicions that I had done exactly what I had done: copied the entire book.

Those notes proved invaluable to me as I fit the whole story together. It was his last entry that shocked me as it rolled off my laser printer. The ink on the diary page must have just dried as he landed in Zurich to see me. The bishop, the prophet, and the Messiah had gathered that morning to discuss the problems with the new European Union. The cementing factor was the Catholic Church, but the pope wasn't in favor of linking politics and the Vatican.

Thompson and Russo felt blocked by this one obstacle in the road to their goal. They couldn't move ahead, and the man sitting in St. Peter's Basilica wouldn't budge on his view. They knew that only one man stood in the way of their establishing the potential and essential power that it would take to solidify the new union on the ashes of the financially broken European Union.

Russo's concern over the clone was more than he had let me know. It was true that Jesus was certainly becoming the leader amongst them. This was disturbing to both Thompson and the bishop. Thompson wanted the Union to come together quickly. He would be airing his show in every one of the countries. The revenue potential was extremely high.

Through my source within the Vatican, I knew that the Holy Father kept the clone at a distance. The pope recognized that any one-on-one meeting would be misconstrued by the Messiah's followers as a validation of the clone's ministry. He still wasn't sure. Something was missing in the clone's brown, piercing eyes. The pope was a most formidable blockade to the plans and desires of the three: the bishop, the prophet and the Messiah.

As I was putting my copy of the diary in a safe place, I noticed one page had been written on hurriedly. The ink lines at times made little sense. I felt like I was reading a thought that Russo needed to remember, a phrasing that was important. Bishop Russo scribbled in large letters,

"He said he would take care of it. What did he mean? Would he…?" The rest was unintelligible. These must have been the last words he scrawled on the airplane before disembarking, hurriedly written after the tension filled morning meeting with the other two. If I conjectured and put together what I read between Russo's words, the clone had exerted himself above them. He had taken on a role above theirs. A role that would one day leave them as his servants. That meeting ended with Jesus saying he would take care of it. He would take care of what? The remaining hours of that day answered the question. It was too shocking to believe, and I suppose when you read it, you won't believe it.

Let no one deceive you by any means; for that Day will not come unless the falling away comes first, and the man of sin is revealed, the son of perdition, who opposes and exalts himself above all that is called God or that is worshiped, so that he sits as God in the temple of God, showing himself that he is God. — II Thessalonians 2:3-4

CHAPTER 12

From my internal Vatican source, I know that the clone met with the pope that evening. It was a quiet and secretive meeting...only a few knew about it. I am indebted to my friend within the Vatican. I don't give a name and I can't give a name, for information comes to me in a variety of ways. Before, it was letters or calls from another person. Once I was in my "safe house" in the California dissenter's center, e-mail was sent via a variety of links. It was impossible to trace me.

I received this letter through a friend. It was lengthy and detailed.

Dear Dr. MacDonald,

I once again raise my pen to write you. I know that you haven't decided to release all that you know at this time. You are the only one who holds most of the keys to this religious puzzle. I think you need this piece as well.

Jesus begged for an audience with the pope. The Holy Father struggled with the idea of legitimizing the clone by a public meeting, and finally agreed to a quiet, clandestine, evening meeting. He did not want his staff to know about it. Only a few of us were aware of its occurrence.

Jesus was very warm and I was shocked by his conversation. What he said so impressed me that it was imbedded in my mind. After the handshake and hug, the Messiah sat down across from the pope and said candidly, "For over thirty years you have struggled against my existence. I can understand that. It is a hard thing to understand why and how I exist. I'm not sure that I have all the pieces myself. All I know is that I am truly Jesus. These are the legs of Jesus and the body of Jesus. My brain has the same capacity. I am created from DNA drawn from my own blood. That blood came from an Immaculate Conception. I am not like other people.

"I want to know why you reject me and turn me away. I want us to work together to bring world peace, to bring prosperity back to this world."

The Holy Father was quiet for a few moments. I imagine he had to think about what was said. He drew in a deep breath and exhaled it over his words. "You have assessed correctly. I believe you do have the body of Jesus, but I feel as if there is something missing. Some special quality that only a true Messiah would have."

The Messiah stared at the pope. There was a very uncomfortable silence before he spoke. "I need to talk with you openly and honestly. May I do that?"

"The Messiah could do nothing else," the Holy Father responded.

"Since my birth, I've been tossed into the bright lights of the media. I've been trained to think like, act like, talk like, and be like a Messiah that no one has ever met. I have memorized the entire Old and New Testaments. All this I've done, but

somehow I feel as if there is something missing in my life," Jesus said to the pontiff.

The Vicar of Christ stood up from his chair. In all their conversations, Jesus had never been so vulnerable. The pope took three steps back from his chair and turned to gaze out the window. With another draw of breath, he spoke to Jesus, "What do you think is missing?"

"I'm not sure. Could I ask His Holiness a question?"

"Yes, please."

"How well do you know Bishop Russo?" Jesus asked.

The question was so unusual that it turned the pontiff's head quickly toward Jesus. He waited a second to respond. "We have been in contact for over thirty-five years. He is very driven and very directed towards the goals that you have set forth."

"You've just hit it. I'm not the one setting the goals. They are."

The pope asked, "Who is this they? Are you referring to Thompson the prophet and the bishop?"

"Yes I am. I feel as if they have been in control of the ministry that I've been sent to this earth to accomplish." Jesus was emphatic.

The pope again sat across from the clone. He leaned forward and touched Jesus's hand. "What is this mission, and who has sent you?"

"My Father and your Father has sent me. I've come so people might have life and have it more abundantly," he said, then paused before finishing his statement. "I've come to finish what I started over two thousand years ago. I've come to bring peace and prosperity to this world."

"So, you truly believe you are the Messiah?" the vicar asked, almost stunned.

"Yes, I am the Messiah. I have come tonight to make peace with you and to help you see that I am the I am. How can I assure you of my genuineness?"

"Your candidness has helped me. Since the beginning, I've felt as if Thompson and Russo had misdirected you. I want our relationship to be closer, but I don't trust your friends. I would like to suggest that we gather each day for prayer. Through our time alone with our Father, we will grow closer together," the Holy Father said.

"Thank you. This has been better than I could have prayed for. May I ask for another favor from His Holiness?"

"Yes, I want us to grow to count on one another."

The clone reached into a bag sitting next to him on the floor. He pulled from it a small vial of wine and circle of bread about two inches across. He laid them before the pontiff and spoke. "Would you take the Holy Eucharist with me?"

The vicar's face broke with a broad smile. "Oh, yes. I would like that."

Jesus took the bread and he broke it, blessed it, and said, "Take. Eat. For this is my body."

He gave a piece to the pope and kept the remainder in his hand. They both lifted the morsels to their mouths and ate.

Jesus then took the small vial of wine and held it up above both of their heads. "Take it and drink, for this is my blood." He offered the vial to the pontiff. The old man drank from the vial and gave it back to Jesus. The Messiah capped the vial and returned it to this bag.

"Are you not going to drink with me?" the pope asked.

"I cannot. For I said in my last visitation to this earth that I would not drink of it again until I partake at the Great Wedding Feast in Heaven, along with the eleven men who walked the roads of Galilee with me. You understand, don't you?" Jesus warmly smiled as he spoke.

"Oh, yes. I can't believe that I forgot your promise to your disciples. Yes, yes, taking the bread is enough. I am honored by that," the pope told him. Then vicar yawned and said that he needed to sleep.

Jesus reached down and pulled his small bag up to him. "Good night. I will look forward to our daily time of prayer."

The pontiff was already walking towards his bedroom. "So am I. I am sorry, but at my age, sleep is greatly needed. Please, excuse me."

At that moment a grayness drifted into the room, filling it like a gigantic shadow laying it's murky, thick foam over the floor. Jesus exited, and I know little else about that meeting. I do hope what I've written has helped.

Signed,

Faithful

These bits of information would mean little except that the next morning brought panic to the vatican. A nun assigned to serve the pontiff would awaken him each morning with a cup of fine Italian coffee. He liked it black. The pope's head would hang over his Bible as he sought God's guidance for the day and for the Holy Roman Catholic Church. He rose early and he rose quickly, like a man that relished each new day with his Lord and God. That morning was quite different.

The nun would usually knock on the door and then enter, setting the pontiff's cup on the ancient mahogany desk in the corner of the room. He would give a kind and soft "thank you" as she departed and went on her other duties. That morning, she placed the cup on the desk and turned to leave. Silence. Nothing was heard. He didn't speak. She turned towards him. The covers were strewn across the bed as if his night had been spent in a struggle. The peaceful face was replaced by twisted agony on the mouth and deep furrows frozen on the brow. She gasped and ran from the room.

"Father Witkowski, come quick! There is something wrong with the Holy Father," she yelled as she pounded on the assistant's thick wooden door. Witkowski stumbled from his bed and opened the door to see the sister's worried face staring at him.

"What is it, sister?" he croaked out in his best early morning voice.

"I took the Holy Father his coffee, as is our ritual each morning. He usually greets me pleasantly and I leave. This morning he said nothing. So, I took a few steps closer. His face has a painful, twisted look on it. Please, come quickly."

They raced down the hall. The noise and voices awoke the others who resided along the passageway. Sensing a serious condition, they bolted through their doorways and followed along the marble floored hall.

Father Witkowski arrived first. He prayed that he would be like the Apostle Peter and enter the room to find his master not there, or that he would see him sitting at his desk deep in study.

As the door opened, the pontiff still lay as the nun had left him, but his face twitched in anguished contortions. His coffee sat steaming on the desk, but no one hovered over it. Father Witkowski knew then that the pope had not passed into the Kingdom of Light. There were signs that the pope was still alive, but what was occurring in his brain seemed evil.

Witkowski turned to the others standing behind him. "Please, stand back. Give me a moment to see what the situation is. I believe His Holiness is still alive. Please, alert the doctor," he begged the others, and then turned to enter the room. The nun was with him.

"Is this how you left him?" Witkowski whispered.

"Yes, Father. This is exactly how I left him," she answered.

"His face is still contorting. There is a sign of life, but I'm not hopeful. Pray, sister!" he said aloud to her as he thought through the situation before him. The contortions on the pontiff's face bewildered him. "Sister, what would cause what we see? I've seen strokes before, I've seen seizures before, but I have never seen this. It's as if he is struggling against an unseen enemy."

"I think he was visited by something evil," she answered as her hands crossed her body in the sign of the cross. She was so close to the truth.

To Witkowski's rational mind, the one thing that brought him to the Vatican, it looked like His Holiness had fought a good fight but lost. Something, someone, some being, some unseen evil had been the victor, and to the victor belonged the spoils.

The dragon gave him his power, his throne, and great authority. — Revelation 13:2

CHAPTER 13

The next day I was awakened very early by a call.

"Matthew?" the voice said.

"Yeah, who is this?" I snapped groggily into the receiver.

"Laura from Prophet Thompson's office."

"Oh, hi Laura. I'm sorry I was a little short with you. What time is it?" I apologized. Laura had continued to be a friend to the family even after my tensions with her boss and Russo began. "What can I do for you? I hope this isn't a call just to chat, because I'll most likely fall asleep on you."

Beth was stirring next to me. The phone had brought her around to the living. She groaned out, "Who is it, Matt?"

"Laura from Thompson's office," I whispered with my hand over the phone.

Laura was starting to talk rapidly. "Did you hear the news? I personally couldn't believe it. What do you think it means? Tom told me yesterday that the clone was meeting with the pope last night."

"Hold it. I don't know what you're talking about. We were out last night, and obviously we were asleep until your call. What is it that is so important that you called us so early?"

"The pope had a stroke last night and is now a contorted vegetable."

"What?" I said loudly as I dropped the phone.

Beth was up on her elbow looking at me. "Matthew, what's going on?"

I tried to quiet her but she was more insistent. "Tell me, please."

"Hold for a second, Laura," I said into the receiver as I turned my upper body to Beth. "The pope had a serious stroke last night."

Beth didn't seem concerned.

"Beth, that's not all. The clone was the last one with him." This caused her to sit straight up. "Laura, what else do you know?" I asked.

"Not much more than that. No reports of mysterious drugs. The doctors surmised it was a stroke, but Maria told me it didn't look that way to her," Laura repeated back.

Maria had spent the early years of Jesus's life with him. Once he was old enough and her usefulness had waned, Russo had dismissed her. The pontiff had put her out of the convent when the clone was born, so she stayed on at the training center. Then, as suddenly as a change in the wind, she was out. The pope was troubled both by his own actions and then Father Russo's, and had asked her to come work at the Vatican. It hadn't taken long before she was allowed to put on the nun's habit again.

"What did she think happened?" I asked Laura.

"She said the pope's face was contorting like he was battling an unseen force. The pope looked like he'd been fighting all night," Laura said anxiously.

"That's interesting," I told her.

"There's one thing more. Tom told me that Jesus is going to speak to the Cardinals and ask them to name Russo the new pope once the inevitable happens. Can you believe that? Johnny Russo could be the next pope."

That news tied my stomach in knots. Nothing would or could stop them now. Step by step I could see their plan building on the previous blocks. Thompson was more powerful than ever. His television shows were more like prime time specials. The prophet had seen the future of cable and the Internet, then expanded into every area possible, including his own social media network and JesusTube. You couldn't turn on the TV without some message from Thompson being on a channel.

Jesus had become the Prince of Peace. The new EU, under his influence, would bring economic and political power to the three of them.

I thought then, *If Russo became the pope then nothing could stop them. Absolutely nothing. They will have brought together the religious, economic, and political power that was great enough to control the world.*

That afternoon I was running errands. I had just been inside my cleaners, and as I exited a figure slid in close to me, whispering, "Come with me. Don't argue. There's a gun in your side." As he said it, my assailant jammed the barrel of a pistol into my kidney. I didn't like it, but then again, I wasn't asked if I liked it or even wanted to obey.

My captor led me around the side of the building along a walkway until we came to a row of automobiles. We approached a black luxury car, and its back door flew open. At the same time my captor's hands pressed down on the back of my head while his other hand shoved me into the car. I stumbled in and dropped at black, wing tipped feet. I looked up. It was him.

"Dr. MacDonald, I'm sorry to have to do that to you," the hard faced man said.

"All this because I spilled a drink on you?" I asked, half joking and half wondering.

"No, no. That isn't it. I didn't want anyone to know that we were meeting. My name is Jack Hesidence, and Doctor, I need your help," he said.

He helped me climb into the seat opposite him in the limousine. "Could you explain yourself a little better? I'm very confused as to why the Director of the C.I.A. would want or need my help."

Hesidence looked startled to find that I knew who he was. "Since the birth of Jesus, I've followed his career. I know where he goes and why he's there; and Dr. MacDonald, I also have had agents tracking you," Hesidence told me.

"Why me? What did I do?"

"You made him, Doctor. You're the man responsible for bringing him to life."

"You say that like I'm Dr. Frankenstein or something," I shot back at him angrily.

"If the shoe fits," he answered.

"Enough of this bantering. What do you want from me?" I insisted.

"We believe that your clone is trying to subvert the world's governments through economics and religion. And by the way, our government leaders aren't the only ones who think so. You might find this hard to believe, but the Russians are scared crapless over this thing.

They've got enough problems with their economy. Your Messiah clone is squeezing their throats so tight their eyes are popping. Everything that we observe leads us to believe that, but we don't have anyone on the inside. We need someone that can get us information before Jesus makes any further moves," he said.

"I don't know anything that's going on. I just made the egg, and now do periodic check-ups. I'm afraid that I can't help you. Now, if you'll excuse me I need to get back to my house," I told Hesidence.

He reached over and opened the door for me. As I slid on the seat towards the door, the director touched my arm and said, "Please, Dr. MacDonald. I believe that your creation will lead us into a world war. One that could destroy us all. Please, consider what I've said. We'll be in touch."

I stepped out of the car and walked to the front of the building, got in my car, and headed home. Beth was standing in the kitchen over a mixing bowl when I strolled in. "You won't believe this, but I think I was just approached to be a spy."

"MacDonald, Matthew MacDonald, double 'O' geneticist with a license to clone," she joked. "Now, tell me the real reason you were late for dinner?"

Then I saw another beast coming up out of the earth, and he had two horns like a lamb and spoke like a dragon. And he exercises all the authority of the first beast in his presence, and causes the earth and those who dwell in it to worship the first beast... — Revelation13:11-12

CHAPTER 14

Soon after the pontiff's reported stroke, the College of Cardinals gathered to decide on how the church would proceed. The men, dressed in their traditional red cloaks, had taken their seats when the clone walked through the door. A large percentage of the cardinals were intense followers of the new Messiah and some had been influenced to the opposite by the recent pope. A few others were more like Russo than anything else. They wanted whatever would uphold themselves in high esteem. The clone had come to speak with them. It was such an important historical moment that a transcript was released of his speech.

The Messiah stood among them, his face filled with sadness. His red, swollen eyes were signs of the hours of weeping that the news had reported...or maybe it was the work of a top level TV make-up artist. He moved slowly between their chairs to one end of the room, where each cardinal could see him. It would be a very important talk, and most likely one of the most pivotal speeches of his life. He looked at each of them and opened his mouth. No words came out, but tears began rolling down his cheeks. Jesus sucked in a breath and wiped his eyes with a slow, methodical stroke of his forefinger.

"I can barely speak. My heart is filled with such emotion that it is blocking my words. Please, bear with me in this difficult moment. I find it difficult to believe that I sat, partaking of the Holy Eucharist with the pontiff only a few days ago. Today, he lies in a coma. The church will soon lose one of its truly great leaders. It will not be easy replacing a man of such grand stature and abilities.

"I do not totally understand all that I am. I have memories from when I walked this earth before. I have a true and sure historical record in the Bible of other things that I said and did, but I don't fully perceive that. In the last few days, a very strong memory has flooded my mind. I was standing with the Apostle Peter, and I asked him, 'Who do you say that I am.' He answered, 'You are the Christ.' I can remember smiling at him, overjoyed that he finally understood and that he'd finally committed totally to me. I said, 'You are Peter, and upon this rock I will build my church.'

"On that day, two thousand years ago, I named the man who would be the first pope. He was the first man to sit in the Chair of Peter. My prayer and desire is that you allow me the opportunity to once again name the person who will sit in the Chair of Peter.

"Today, there is only one man of God that can fill the sandals and the chair vacated by so many great men of faith through the centuries. He is a man of great foresight. He is a man of tremendous spiritual strength, and he

THE SIGN OF THE END

serves his god. Bishop John Russo is my choice. No, it's better to say, upon this rock of John Russo, I will continue building my church."

Applause rose from the College of Cardinals. The sleeves of their red garments flapped like so many red winged birds. Jesus stepped down and slowly but intently walked towards the door. He greeted, shook hands with, and hugged many of those men sitting along the aisle in the marble lined room. As he reached the door, the clone turned to the cardinals and said, "I leave you to your very difficult task of choosing a leader for my church. It might be today or it might be in a few weeks, but we know it will soon be your task to decide. Thank you for your time. May my Father in Heaven guide you." He wept again and exited the room.

The speech was marvelous, but the distrust of Russo by some of the dissenting priests was even greater. The College of Cardinals had to wait for their vote on a new pope. Their recognized leader, Archbishop Carello, stood amongst his brothers in the faith and explained how trying this time was, and that they should use the future days to fast and pray. Very few would take his advice, for they had already decided to follow the clone's guide.

Suspicions varied within and without the Vatican and the church at large. A few suspected foul play. Others believed it was a manipulation of Jesus by Russo. A few more wanted to see Johnny Russo assume the throne as Pope Simon Peter, and the sooner the better. Instead, Carello convinced them to wait.

To appease Russo and to show the world their support for the words of the Messiah, a letter to the Holy Roman Catholic Church was written. It simply said that in this trying and difficult time, the College of Cardinals was

105

seeking God's guidance and needed time to read, pray, and fast. In the interim, Bishop Russo would assume the reins of the church until the pontiff passed and a new pope was selected.

I was glad I wasn't around when Russo found out about that. His reaction would have been like Hell visiting itself upon earth.

Little children, it is the last hour; and as you have heard that the Antichrist is coming — I John 2:18

CHAPTER 15

Russo didn't have the only reaction to the news. The greatest thing about the modern communication system was that I could watch United States news anytime I wanted it. I flipped on the TV that day and channel surfed until I came across the following report. I pressed the DVR button and recorded it. Later, I had my secretary transcribe it. I was not sure why. I guess I was keeping different things in my scrapbook and I thought it would be a nice addition.

NEWSCASTER: "The news of the Catholic church's delay in their election of a new pope brought strong reaction in our country today. Wall Street saw a plummet of over three thousand points, and religious groups went to battle."

INTERVIEW WITH PRIEST: "I'm not sure if they did the right thing at all. Once again we see our church leaders ignoring the will of the people and assuming that they know everything. If Jesus said that Bishop Russo should be pope, then that is exactly how it should be. It is time for the cardinals to make some changes in how things are done. The pope is in a coma and is not coming out. Let's move on."

NEWSCASTER: "And in the same church, the monsignor cautioned us about criticizing the cardinals."

MONSIGNOR: "They are following the path that has church tradition and the church fathers behind it. They chose to do it this way in order to protect the office of the pope and the church. I personally believe that Jesus is the real Christ, but I need to follow along with my spiritual overseers."

CHRISTIAN: "I'm a Christian and I don't see how this would affect my life. We don't follow the pope, and I certainly don't want to get involved in their problems."

NEWSCASTER: "But the far right pastor of that woman's church preaches a different message from the doorway of his small building."

PASTOR: "Calvary is an independent and fundamental church. We don't recognize the leadership of the pope, but we do recognize that Christ is the head of the church...the real Christ, not this cloned one. Instead of recognizing a new pope, Catholics need to recognize that they need a savior and accept Jesus into their hearts, today."

NEWSCASTER: "In Colorado, a group from the Universal Way, an all-inclusive church, had a saner and more Christlike view."

CHURCH LEADER: "Jesus is one of our Ascended Masters. Now, in his current manifestation, we find true comfort in what he says and does. If Bishop Russo becomes the leader of the Holy Catholic Church, then I believe there will be tremendous harmony amongst the spiritual energies of people across the universe. That

108

harmony will bring all religions together under one leader, Jesus the Messiah."

NEWSCASTER: "But the most frightening reaction comes from a militia styled group in California. Their spokesperson, Clint Cole, said in an official statement that their 'followers view the clone as a dangerous tool being used by the world governments to take away people's freedoms.' Cole further stated that they plan to move to their well concealed camps and wait for the coming world war. Even something as good and peaceful as a Messiah can bring out the worst in people."

The newscast switched to another topic and I leaned back in the easy chair of my den. At that point I wasn't sure what was happening. Jesus was the last one to be with the pope, who'd had a reported stroke that night that appeared not to be a stroke to those who were eye witnesses. I'd had my suspicions at the time, but there was no proof.

When the clone asked for Russo to be elected pope, I thought I saw the purpose in it. If Russo controlled the world's largest religious group, and with Thompson's tremendous sway in the U.S. Protestant community, they could easily milk more cash out of the church groups and world governments. At least, that was what I thought was behind the whole mess. I never imagined that the clone was truly behind the decision to eliminate the pope.

With all the religious upheaval and strife in the North American churches, Russo and Thompson convinced Jesus that he needed to make a peace trip. He was scheduled to meet with the heads of every major denomination and religious group. I got a call from Thompson a few days before the trip.

"Matty, old boy, this is Reverend T. N. T. How ya doin'?" His voice boomed through my phone. Preachers never got off the podium. His joviality took me by surprise. The prophet often talked down-home with me, but rarely was that friendly.

"Prophet Thompson, what can I do for you?" I responded, hoping not to show my surprise.

"How many times do I have to tell you, call me Tom? Anyway, Johnny and I were thinking that it has got to be time that you took that pretty wife of yours on a vacation," he said.

"Actually, that was exactly what she told me just a few weeks ago," I answered in amazement.

"They don't call me the prophet for nothin'," he laughed.

"What do you have in mind?" I asked.

"How about Disney World?"

"I haven't been there in years. Not since Cari was still at home. I'll bet Beth would like that, but what's the occasion?" I inquired.

"There's a lot of ballyhoo over there with the churches and different religious groups. So, Johnny's bringin' your little creation to America to have a pow-wow with them. I guess he doesn't believe that I've got the sway with the religious community that my TV ratings say I do." He paused to take a silent dissenting breath and then continued. "But that's not the important part. We want you to join us, and maybe while you're there you can do a little check-up on Jesus," Thompson told me.

"Is there something wrong with him?" I asked with deep concern.

"He's had a lot of strain and stress on him since his dearest and closest friend, the pope, became seriously ill."

I laughed to myself. Did he think that I still had hayseed on my shoulders? He wasn't talking to one of his back road farm congregants. I hardly caught the next part, the prophet spoke so fast.

"I think that the rejection, or delay rather, of his call for John to be elected to the position took its toll on him. Come on down to Florida and relax for a bit. You can stay here at my house. I'll have Laura get things ready," the prophet offered.

"Sounds great. I'll talk to Beth and then give you a call back. Hey, and tell Laura that Beth and I send our love."

We hung up. I had hoped that I didn't give away how I really felt during the conversation. I thought quickly through all that had happened since Russo came to see me and had dropped his diary. Thompson and the bishop had wanted me to examine the clone and had figured a way to get me to do it. Actually, I was anxious to examine him and discover a little more information.

A few days later, Beth and I found ourselves laying in the hot Florida sun next to Thompson's pool, which had been built in the shape of a cross. It was tacky, but he held baptisms in it for his TV show. The prophet was very creative in his methods of making a profit and staving off taxes. Every luxury became a write-off. He always said that the less Uncle Sam got, the more the Lord got. I guessed the Lord was letting Thompson hold it all in escrow for a time. I was often reminded of his favorite joke. "I throw the offering in the air and tell the Lord to take what He wants."

A voice called to me and I popped my eyes open to see Laura, Thompson's personal assistant and full-time lover. "Matt, I had one of the servants pull a car around to the front for you. He left the keys in it. Don't forget that

Bishop Russo and Jesus the Messiah will be here for dinner around six," Laura reminded me.

Beth joined the conversation. "How did their meetings go?"

"Tom was very pleased. Most of the bishops were very receptive to Jesus, and groups like the Universal Way embraced him as their spiritual leader while encouraging their brothers and sisters of every faith to do the same. I'm pretty sure that Jesus has turned the tide, except for those religious extremists. I always thought we were supposed to be one in Christ," she sneered as she told Beth before walking back into the house to make preparations for dinner. I was close behind her and heading to my room to change clothes before leaving.

I pulled out of the prophet's complex and headed down Tangerine Drive towards Orlando. The road was lined with tall, majestic, royal palms. I liked the royal the most out of the selection of palm trees in Florida because of their massive trunk and height. I was sure that the original Jesus rode between trees like them when the crowds cried out, "Hosanna, blessed is he who comes in the name of the Lord." Of course, one week later they yelled in bloodthirsty voices, "Crucify him!"

Right after I turned onto Ocean Boulevard a car pulled from the side of the road and slid in behind me. I went several blocks with my eyes glancing up at the mirror every few seconds. On one of my looks at the road, I noticed that the traffic signal up ahead was yellow. I hoped that I could make it through before the thing turned red. If I made it, I could shake the car tailing me.

I blasted into the intersection as the light turned and gunned the car down Ocean Boulevard. The black car with tinted windows whipped through behind me. I heard horns blaring at the car, followed by the sound of screeching tires. I looked up and the vehicle was bearing down on me again. I slid around the next corner and punched the gas. My borrowed car left long, black strips of rubber on the pavement.

I made it to the next corner, but couldn't maneuver the bend and slid against the curb. I heard a loud pop and the car started limping along. I knew I had blown a tire, so I slammed on the brakes. By the time I came to a stop my pursuer was already next to me. The doors of the car flew open and two men in suits yanked my door open. Large hands grabbed me, and my body followed them into the bright Orlando sun. The next thing I knew, I was in the back seat of the large black car with tinted windows.

When He opened the fifth seal, I saw under the altar the souls of those who had been slain for the word of God and for the testimony which they held. And they cried with a loud voice, saying, "How long, O Lord, holy and true, until You judge and avenge our blood on those who dwell on the earth?" — Revelation 6:9-10

CHAPTER 16

"So, we meet again, Doctor."

"Hesidence, why did you do that? And why are you here? Or even better, how did you know that I was going to be here?" I growled at the C.I.A. Director.

"C'mon now, Doctor, this is the C.I.A. We should be able to find out little things like your whereabouts and your schedule. Besides, I needed to talk to you, and it had to be alone and away from the prophet's compound. Don't worry about the tire, my agents are putting on the spare for you," he said as his face went from a friendly smile to a concerned frown. I sat quietly and nodded at him to go on. "First of all, I want to remind you that I am interested in information concerning the Messiah you made."

"Listen, Director, you are really starting to irritate me. I cloned some DNA and out of it came a man. That man is

Jesus. There was no crime in what I did, and I wish you would quit talking to me like I did something wrong," I snapped at him.

The smile came back across his face. "You're right, Matt. I'm sorry. It is still the feelings of the agency that Jesus is planning something that could affect the wellbeing of this nation and many others. We need help."

"There's nothing I can say," I told him as I pulled my eyes away from his. My mind struggled with what he'd said. Was it just the paranoid pipe-dreams of a government agency that had outlived its usefulness? Or was he right? Had I created the beast that Hesidence believed Jesus to be?

"I understand, Doctor. Let me go on to the second subject. As you know, there are several groups that do not feel that Jesus is the Messiah. Many of them are part of the dissenter's movement. Two of those groups are planning to assassinate Jesus on his way to Disney World tomorrow. One group is out of Georgia, with strong Klan connections that could make them very dangerous. The other one is from the northern and central sections of Florida. Both groups are tough enough to rip off your head and spit down your neck," Hesidence said.

"Thanks for the graphic description. I can't figure out what you want me to do. One geneticist against a bunch of psycho soldier wannabees can't do much. If I could have gotten to them before birth I might have been able to alter their brains so they could have used them, but I'm afraid I'm powerless once a person goes beyond a single gene," I argued.

"We'll take care of the dissenters. I just want you to delay the departure time so I can get my decoys in place."

"Couldn't you just tell Bishop Russo? He'd change the whole thing if he knew the seriousness of the situation," I said.

"I don't want Russo, Thompson, or Jesus to know what's going on. I would prefer that they had no idea how closely we are watching them. Besides, if the dissenters know your schedule, then they have an informant in the mansion. Can you delay him about fifteen minutes until we get our people in place ahead of you?" Hesidence requested.

I nodded my head yes and the director pushed the door open. I exited and climbed back into my borrowed car. I was too shaken to continue my trip, but I was also sure that my quick return would bring too many questions. I forced myself to continue as planned.

The next morning, the whole household got up early and prepared for our Disney adventure. I swear, most of them were acting like little kids getting ready to meet Mickey Mouse. Several times during the preparations, I needed to excuse myself. My stomach was killing me. The stress of knowing what was going to happen left me with a slight case of diarrhea. Moments before we left, another attack sent waves of nausea through me. At first I cursed the ache inside me, until it struck me that I had the perfect excuse to save Jesus's life.

The cars had been brought around to the front. Everyone climbed into one or the other of the two limousines, and I was the last one to enter. The moment I stuck my head in the car, I stopped and spoke to the others. "I'm sorry. This is terribly embarrassing, but I need to run to the bathroom again. Maybe you should all go on without me."

It was Thompson who responded true to form. "No way, Matthew. We can wait while a guy takes care of business. I don't think that Mickey will close the place down if we aren't there exactly on time. A few minutes won't hurt at all."

My stall was all that Director Hesidence needed. Two identical limos to the ones we were riding in pulled out from around the corner and assumed our pathway to the park. What happened never hit the papers, but Hesidence let me in on the details in a later meeting.

The lead limousine would have been the one I was in, and the following car would have carried Jesus, Russo, Laura, and Thompson. The limos we were in were not armored. Bullets could have riddled the glass and metal, driving home death blows to Jesus and the others in the car.

The dissenter's plan was fairly simple: they were to pick off the limousines as they passed. My first reaction was that the C.I.A. simply needed to arrest the shooters. What I didn't know was that there were several possible hit sites, and Hesidence wasn't sure which one they would use. He needed to draw their fire with identical decoys of our vehicles. I thought it ironic that a clone would have his life spared by a clone of another type.

As the decoys took the regular route to Disney World from the Prophecy Center, an assassin was spotted on the First National Bank roof. Hesidence's agents moved in and eliminated him. Over the route there were six other attempts, and all were thwarted. In two cases, shots were fired before agents captured the shooters. Had we been on that route, we would have been dead.

Meanwhile, our two limos pulled out of the estate and found an Orlando police officer in the middle of the street.

She told us, "We're sorry, but there's been an accident up ahead and we're rerouting traffic. I'd suggest Okeechobee Boulevard for the next few blocks, and then to the highway."

Beth stuck her head out the window and asked, "Is anyone hurt? Maybe we can help." In her mind, I imagine she was thinking of the Messiah's miraculous powers. Not that I had ever seen them work in the realm of healing of accident victims, but Beth was still believing on and off that Jesus could be the real thing. I was getting more serious doubts by the day.

"No, ma'am. Everyone is fine but the street is filled with disabled vehicles." With that the police officer turned back to her post. We took Okeechobee Boulevard as instructed and arrived at Disney World about a half hour behind schedule.

Disney's usual proficiency moved us quickly into the theme park and onto Main Street, U.S.A. There was enough of a Disney personnel bubble around the Messiah and the rest of us to keep the crowds from pressing in. In many ways this was one of the funniest sights I had ever seen...Jesus walking down the streets of Disney World with his mouth hanging open, staring at the man-made wonders. I believed that I saw the little child come out in him. That kid-like innocence that Bishop Russo had robbed from him was racing from his eyes and gushing out in the "ooos" and "ahhs" he constantly uttered.

We had just exited Main Street and turned right to head up the small hill by the food stand and then into the Future. The prophet thought it would be the perfect photo op to have himself and Jesus standing in Future Land. I hadn't taken more than five steps into the future when I was surrounded by the Seven Dwarfs, all jabbering and talking away. The others had stopped to watch while the horde herded me away from them.

I was getting irritated at these cartoon escapees when one of them, Grumpy, leaned in close and said, "Doctor, please come with me. Director Hesidence is waiting for you in the Enchanted Castle."

"Tell him that I am here with my wife and don't want to play his silly, secret agent games," I barked back as I pushed Grumpy out of my way. But Grumpy pushed back at me and growled, "This is not a request, and I'm not that excited about being dressed in this hot, ridiculous costume. So don't make a sweet little cartoon character beat the tar out of you and drag you along the miserable walkway."

Grumpy was grumpy enough, but when he flipped out and threatened to pound me I quickly smiled and said, "After you, dwarfs. Is the director dressed as Snow White?" I called to the others to go on into Future Land while I traveled with my seven favorite diminutive friends to find the facilities.

Hesidence stood inside the door that went up to the castle's restaurant. He was casually dressed in a Mickey T-shirt, sunglasses, ugly plaid Bermuda shorts, and a camera swung around his neck. I would've laughed except that there were probably a hundred other men in the park dressed with much poorer taste.

"Matthew, I'm sorry for having to bring you to me this way. It does seem a little like overkill, but I needed to get you away without any suspicion. I have to seek your help again."

"What now?"

"We found out from one of the militia men that we captured that the groups had a fail-safe. One of them is here in the park. He is their best trained man in every area of weapons and explosives," Hesidence grunted.

"It's like that in every movie, isn't it? Can't you come up with some other story that isn't so tired and lame?"

"Matt, listen to me. This is not a story. He's on a suicide mission. The kook is wired with enough explosives to take out Jesus and all his entourage. That includes Beth. Now, if you don't want to help, that's okay," Hesidence said as he looked into my eyes with his piercing, cold stare. He knew that mentioning Beth would be enough to win my agreement.

"What do you need me to do?" I asked.

"Get your whole group outta here," he snapped.

"And how do I do that?" was my response.

"Take this." Hesidence pulled a small pill from his pocket and showed it to me in his extended palm.

"What? Are we back in a bad spy movie again? I suppose this little pill will make me look like I'm having a heart attack," I scoffed in his face.

"Yeah, you're right. Now, take it so we can end this visit to the fantasy world before it ends your world." He pushed it closer to me and I picked it out of his hand. Grumpy shoved a bottle of designer water in my other hand.

"Hesidence, what happens if this wacko catches up to us before you catch up to him? What do you want me to do, dance with him?" I asked sarcastically.

"Yeah, MacDonald, dance with him. Now, don't be such a wise guy, and get your friends out of here," Hesidence retorted as he pulled his walkie-talkie to his ear.

I caught up with the group a few minutes later. I already felt the effects of the pill. My head dropped down to look at my watch. In another ten minutes, I'd drop to the ground with a sudden pain down my arm. I moved close to Beth and whispered, "I can't explain what's going to happen to me in the next few minutes, but no matter what—don't worry."

She looked stunned and tried asking questions, but I put my finger to my lips. Her eyes were filled with worry. Isn't worry the craziest thing? We tell someone not to worry and the first thing they do is worry. Beth worried. I tried to relieve her beforehand but I failed. I ended up extending the worry period for her.

In five minutes, the pains started slowly and with slight intensity. They would increase, I knew it. I moved in closer to Jesus with a grimace on my face. Each time a pain struck I flinched. He noticed it.

"Matt, what's the problem? Is your stomach acting up again? Do we need to get you to a toilet?" he joked. I was about to say that I felt pains coming down my arm when I looked up. I stared at my old friend Grumpy, who was walking away from the kid's rides in Fantasy Land towards us. We were only a few steps from Space Mountain. I grinned at my dwarf friend. I had to laugh when I thought of the grouchy attitude of the agent inside the Grumpy costume. It was very appropriate. Then another pain hit.

I was ready to say something when Grumpy got closer. I thought I'd give him a little of his own medicine and drag the character into my heart attack scene. I stepped away from Jesus and walked toward Grumpy. "Grumpy, my old friend, it's so good to see you again." I threw my arms out and hugged him. They wrapped around the costume.

"Get off me, jerk," Grumpy said in character, but there were two things wrong. The voice was different, and Grumpy was carrying some extra baggage strapped to his chest. Then the thought struck me…this was the assassin and I had my arms around him. In another three minutes, I would crumble to the ground in intense pain. It was lousy timing. I had the killer in my grasp, but I had one hundred and eighty seconds to let the C.I.A. know or to take the militia madman out on my own.

Another pain hit and another few seconds ticked by. What could I do? I felt like I was Doctor McCoy on Star Trek and I should be saying, "Jim, I'm a doctor, not a government agent." But when the next pain hit, I knew I had to react quickly or Beth's life might be endangered.

What could I do? Then I remember saying, "Hesidence, what should I do, dance with him?" That was it. The pains were coming constantly, but I had to dance. I needed to dance to save my life, my wife's life, and my friends' lives. I pulled my arms away from the bomber and grabbed his two hands, and screamed, "Let's dance!"

My Arthur Murray lessons came in handy. I moved my aching body into a waltz. Grumpy was trying not to give himself away to the others, but I've got to say that he wasn't whispering sweet nothings in my ear as we twirled around on our paved dance floor. I was taking another spin when someone smashed my chest with a sledgehammer. I spasmed away from him and fell at his feet. The dance had ended. I had failed.

Things started to go black and I faded from the scene. It was strange to have been in the midst of all that action and only know the events by what I was told and what I saw on the news. A woman was shooting a video of her family and had moved the camera to capture some shots of Jesus. Her video was all I saw from that point on, because I was out cold.

When I fell, Beth screamed. The assassin didn't have a chance to move before the C.I.A. grabbed him and whisked him into the underground system beneath Disney World.

The next thing I remember was the back of an ambulance. I expected to see Beth's face leaning over mine, but what I got was the icy, deep lined face of Jack Hesidence. "Matt, wake up. The antidote should be working by now."

"Antidote?" I mumbled.

"Without the antidote you could have died," Hesidence filled me in.

"I'm glad you told me that. I just wish you would have said it before and I might not have done it."

The director smiled and said, "That's why I didn't tell you before." He patted me on the shoulder and smiled again. His smiles were so rare that I was surprised that I had gotten two of them. "Doctor MacDonald, we got our man because of you. For a second, I couldn't imagine what you were doing dancing with Grumpy. Then when one of the other agents asked why you were dancing, it hit me. You said it as a joke, but it was the signal we needed to move in and take the suicide bomber down. The most unusual one I've seen in all my years of service, but pretty smart. What you did was very brave. That was a lot more than we asked of you."

"I did it for my wife, so don't pull out any medals yet." I sucked in a breath. I was starting to gain my strength and my concentration back. Enough of my mind had gained alertness at that point for me to I ask the C.I.A. Director, "If my clone is such a danger to world peace and prosperity, then why didn't you let one of the assassins take him out?"

"That isn't the way we do things, Matt. Besides, a murdered religious leader creates a martyr. Martyrs are much tougher to stop than a living Messiah. I need him alive so I can prove that he's a fake. You might even have that proof, and that's why you keep seeing my face," Hesidence answered.

"Look at all the great things that he's done in the world. Why do you want to prove he's a fake?" I asked.

"His political connections are building allied armies so large that the balance of power is growing out of balance. The most frightening thing about it is that these countries will no longer be led by their elected officials. The real power will be in a man made from DNA— debated not to be the real Jesus—a power hungry priest, and a man that hears voices from God. You tell me, is that what you want for the world?" Hesidence stopped talking. I knew he was emotionally bothered by the world's situation, but wasn't sure that I agreed with him on the causes.

By the time the ambulance pulled up in front of the hospital, I was feeling fine. Beth ran to the back doors of the vehicle as they were opening. I saw the shock on her face as I sat up and greeted her with a big smile and said, "It was indigestion. They gave me some baking soda in water and I'm fine."

We hugged and she whispered, "Will you please tell me now what is going on around this place?"

"In time, hon, in time."

At Thompson's mansion, Laura intercepted me when I walked through the front door. She said, "Jesus wants to talk to you. He wants to offer his deepest thanksgiving for what you did for all of us. He's upstairs laying down in his room."

"Why is he in bed?" I asked, concerned.

"He complained of a pain in his side, his hands and feet were going numb, and he has a ring of stabbing pain around his head. He didn't look well," Laura answered. He had never been sick for even a second in all the years since his birth. What was happening? My body chilled with an icy shiver. I shook and looked up the stairs in time to see a shadow move slowly along the landings wall, heading for the clone's suite.

A man's days are numbered. You know the number of his months. He cannot live longer than the time You have set.
— *Job 14:5*

CHAPTER 17

After that day at Disney World, Jesus recovered quickly and was back to his regular schedule as far as I knew. But I knew little for the next several months. Orlando was my last physical contact with Jesus, Thompson, or Russo for a while. But I knew what they were doing on the international scene. It was spoken about on every TV station, written about in every paper, and discussed in every pub.

Jesus continued cementing together the new European Union. The world around him was crying out for peace and prosperity. Nation after nation agreed to his peace proposals, and the economies grew.

Thompson's satellite system beamed his show into every home on the globe, and Bishop Russo remained Bishop Russo. There were still two cardinals that strongly opposed his ascension to the highest position in the Church. The first was a Polish man with strong dignity and pride. I had met him once, years ago, in Rome, and we'd conversed in several different languages. It became a test to see which of us spoke the most tongues. He won. If it had been my choice, he would have been pope and John Russo would still be in some small Chicago parish away from power and away from the Vatican.

Russo's influence over the world's largest grouping of Christian people was frightening to me. Probably because so many people of the faith never listened to what was being said or saw what was being done. They just followed. If anything would bring this world to the brink of Armageddon, it would be our inability to see beyond the sound bites and beyond the slick marketing.

That was precisely what worried me at that time. People were not seeing beyond those things. The prophet's smooth voice and digital images showed the world only what the three of them wanted it to know about themselves and about world leaders.

When Spain's head of state, Pietro Montoya, dissented, a feature news story on one of Thompson's programs showed video clips of Montoya propositioning young children for sex. No matter how much he denied it and said the photos weren't of him, no one believed him. Why should they? Would a man of the cloth lie? More honestly, I had come to believe that the more outlandish the accusations were, the easier people believed it. Like my dad used to say, "The bigger the fish story, the easier it is for people to swallow it."

Russo and Thompson destroyed everyone in their way. Over those months, I grew more frightened of the power the world placed in the hands of Jesus, his priest, and his prophet. They had become like an unholy trinity to me. I wished to have no contact with any of them.

My wish was denied. The cold air of January blew Bishop Russo into my office one more time. His usual smile didn't come with him. There was a problem.

"John, you look bad. What's happening?"

"The prophet and I have been watching Jesus. He's been sick often, and his energy drains quickly from him. There is something wrong," Russo explained.

"Give me more details. What exactly are the symptoms?" I said, as if I was a medical doctor instead of a geneticist.

"It happens once a week and it last for about three days, beginning with an intense headache. I've seen him groan in agony over it. If he's walking when it hits, his body falls to its knees as if pushed from behind. Then his extremities go numb. He says he can't feel his hands and feet. His head hurts, but his feet and hands are numb," Russo said.

"Anything else?"

"Yeah, you better believe there's more. He gets a sharp pain in his side like appendicitis, but we've had that checked out. Doctors can't find a darned thing wrong with him, but like clockwork the pains start until his breathing becomes labored and almost painful to watch. His body spasms just to catch its breath. Finally, he falls asleep...or more appropriately, it's like a coma. Then three days after it starts, he springs from the bed like a young boy." Russo sank back deep into my guest chair and exhaled.

"There's one thing more. I always know when it's about to happen. It's as if the whole room dims...." Russo stopped. His eyes watched something move along the wall behind me. They widened until the whites filled up with fear, an intense fear. He dropped his head.

"You were saying...."

"Nothing, it was nothing. It was probably just my imagination. Can you see him, Mac?" the bishop requested.

"I'm not a medical doctor," I responded.

"I've been to medical doctors. I want to know if there is some kind of genetic break down," Russo answered as his eyes pleaded with me.

The last thing I wanted was to be back in close contact with the three of them. They were bad enough, but when those three came near me, Hesidence usually showed up. I struggled with my answer but finally agreed. I needed to do it for science. I was the leading man in genetics and the only one with a successful clone still functioning. Jesus may be the link to what had caused the other failed experiments.

"When can you bring him here?" I asked.

"How about Friday morning? He's due for another attack somewhere in that time, and it might be helpful if you can see him when he's going through it. Please, don't let anyone else know what's happening," Russo begged as he stood to leave.

"I won't."

He left me and I noticed that the sky was dimming. It was nearly dusk and I wanted to be home early. Beth and I had planned dinner with friends and I'd promised I wouldn't stay late at the office. I tried not to say a word through our evening out, but that was most likely the greatest cause of my wife's questioning.

"Matthew, what is wrong? You've been out of it all night. Is your mind wandering somewhere?" she pressed.

I tried to avoid her question and walk away. "Nothing's wrong."

"Russo?" She barked the question like the name was a curse.

"What?" I grunted

"It was Russo. He called or stopped by or something. What happened? What did that bas—guy want now?" she questioned, with fury in her eyes and voice.

"I'm not very good at hiding things from you, am I?"

"After all these years why do you try? Besides, you make it too easy. You get that confused professor look on your face, and it stays until you discuss what's on your mind. So, discuss it so I can get my Matthew MacDonald back," Beth said as she rubbed the back of her soft hand on my drawn cheek.

"The clone's body is starting to fail. It sounds like it's the same thing that happened to him in Orlando when we were there. I'll have to see him. I don't want to be involved, but this one's for science," I said to her.

"Creating him was for science as well. Look what happened. You have the pope near death, the C.I.A. watching your every move, crazy militia men trying to kill us, and all because you did a great work for science. Stay out of it this time, Matt. Just stay away!" Beth's voice raised slowly in its inflection. By the time her syllables struck "stay away" Beth was screaming at me. She jammed her feet into the steps on the staircase and then slammed the door to our bedroom. I was even more confused.

I sat rubbing my face with my hands when I heard a slight tapping on the front door. It startled me and I snapped my body up from the couch. I was afraid to see who it was. I crept slowly to the foyer and moved back the curtain. I rubbed the moisture from the window to make a peephole. Instead, I ended up looking at someone's eye. I rubbed further to expose Hesidence's face.

I opened the door and stepped onto the porch with him. "Why are you here? Can't a guy have a war with his wife in peace?"

"*War and Peace*, I get it, funny. That was quite a fight. What was it all about? It couldn't have been anything to do with Bishop Russo's visit today, could it?" Hesidence said through his smug smile. He was constantly letting me know that the C.I.A. was aware of my every move.

"It's none of your business what we fought about or what Russo wanted. Leave me alone, I'm going to bed." I stepped back inside and closed the door tightly.

I heard him on the other side saying, "I hope that couch is comfortable."

Beth and I talked little over the next two days. Thompson and Russo arrived early Friday morning and came directly to my office from their hotel rooms.

Thompson began the talking. "Matty, this is one heckuva problem we're all facing. Jesus is getting universal acceptance as the Son of God, and all of a sudden his body is going haywire on us. You created this thing; don't you have a warranty or something on him?"

"Matthew, please come see him and find out what the problem is. There are a lot of souls riding on him," Russo said, but was interrupted by the prophet.

"And there's a lot of money riding on it as well. We need your help," Reverend Thompson pleaded.

I pulled a few instruments together and we walked to their waiting limousine. The driver headed for the hotel. When I finally saw my creation, Jesus was lying still in the dark with a cold cloth on his brow. I lifted it and he opened his eyes to see who it was.

"Doctor, what's wrong? Why do I hurt like this?"

"That's what I'm trying to find out. I've got to take some blood and skin tissue. I'll examine those and see what's happening inside the cells. I'm sure it's something simple to fix with the right combination of vitamins and minerals. Just relax and we'll get these samples and I'll let you rest again," I told the clone.

He gave me a weak smile and I dropped the cloth back on his forehead. I could see why the other two were so concerned. He looked as if he was struggling for his life. His breath came in spasmed gasps, and some pains would double Jesus up into a ball. His agony was more than I could watch.

The entire room felt heavy as I sat and watched my experiment pass through his convulsions. The curtains were pulled and the lights were out. It was dark except for the shaft of light I had slicing from the partially opened bathroom door.

I had rested my eyes for a few moments. The strain was giving me a skull-banging headache as well. I felt something on my neck that sent a shiver along my spine while the skin on my entire body raised in goose bumps. I was suddenly aware of another presence in the room. I hadn't heard Thompson or Russo enter, and I never heard any steps, but there was definitely a presence. Whoever, or whatever, it was made my body shiver like the cold of a wet, damp cave. My eyes darted around the room. There was nothing there. Nothing. But I felt something. I couldn't hear the breath, but I felt its hot moisture against my neck. My body shivered again.

For we do not wrestle against flesh and blood, but against principalities, against powers, against the rulers of the darkness of this age, against spiritual hosts of wickedness in the heavenly places. — Ephesians 6:12

CHAPTER 18

I swiveled around in the chair and shot my eyes to the wall behind me, then stood and took two steps when out of the darkness came a hard, unseen punch to my chest. Stumbling backwards, I crashed over the arm of my chair before spilling to the floor and rolling over, dazed, but more than that, my mind was petrified with fear.

I pulled myself up until I was on my knees by the bed and looked around again, but still couldn't see my assailant. Who or what had hit me? I tried to stand, but felt this great weight pressing down on my shoulders, slamming me back to my knees. My eyes rolled upward, and this time I saw something. A shadow raced across the bed and smashed into my body, hurling me into the hardwood legs of the chair this time. Unsteadily I stumbled to my feet, coughing from the blast and spattering blood.

The shadow moved to the bed again and then over the Messiah. I caught my breath and gasped out, "What are you?"

Immediately the shadow dropped on top of the clone and he sprang up straight in the bed, whipping his head around to stare at me with glowing eyes. In a growling voice, the Messiah said, "I am your god," then fell back to the bed.

I leaped over the back of my chair, raced across the floor, and pulled the door open. Thompson and Russo were on the balcony, so they couldn't have heard or caused what had transpired. Truthfully, I couldn't have explained it either. All I knew was that I was scared. I was real scared.

I spent the next day replaying the events from the room and examining my samples from Jesus to discover the cause of the unusual ailments. It wasn't until about eleven o'clock at night that I discovered a very unusual breakdown in the DNA that was being produced in the new cells that the body creates daily. Jesus's body was killing him.

I picked up my phone and punched in Russo's hotel number. "John, I think I've found the problem. Can you and Reverend Thompson come over right away?" He grunted, "Yes," and clicked the phone down. I expected them in the next half hour. That would give me enough time to pull my notes together and decide what I wanted to tell them. It was time that they heard exactly what I felt.

When their knock came on my office door, I slid from the desk and pulled it open. Both men had hopeful looks in their eyes. I hated to hit them with the undeniable truth. "Sit down. This is going to take us a few minutes to discuss."

"What is it, Matt? Don't do this. We want to know now." Russo jumped out at me.

"Okay, I'll do it as simply as possible and then you can ask some questions. Each new cell that Jesus's body creates to replace the ones that normally die off in a body has alterations in the DNA code. They are sending out signals that give him the headaches, pains, and even the body shut down. Eventually, enough changes will occur that the body will shut down totally," I explained.

"Die? Are you saying that he's dying?" Russo blurted.

"Yes. That is exactly what I'm saying."

It was Thompson that said more. "It can't be. We're not ready for this. He can't die now."

Russo glanced at Thompson and he composed himself. The bishop then turned to me and asked, "Exactly how long do we have?"

"That is one thing that I don't know. It could be another year or two. It could be a few months from now," I answered.

"Then he has a lot of work to do if our Messiah is going to unify the many faiths of this world," Russo told me.

"That's the other thing that I wanted to talk to you about. It's bothered me for a long time, and in the last three years my apprehension has grown." Both of my old partners in the clone project leaned back and glanced at each other as I continued. "Quite a few things made me question what's going on. I guess I should begin at the beginning. When we entered into this project, I was doing it for science and, I admit, for the money. I always knew that I could do it, but I failed to ask if I should do it. Cloning a human is one thing, but cloning the body used by God on this earth was something completely different.

137

Then over the years, I started to get the feeling that Jesus was lacking some very important elements."

Thompson leaned forward and brought his face close to mine. "Like what, Doctor?" Russo stuck out his arm and pulled the prophet back into his seat.

"To begin with, I don't feel like he has…this may sound stupid, but I don't think he has a soul."

"Who do you think you are? You're nothing but some scientist who thinks that his bio specimen is bad. You keep to science and I'll handle the soul stuff," Thompson exploded.

"I'm sorry, Prophet Thompson. I wasn't trying to downgrade your years of education and experience in the ministry. I was merely giving my assessment. An experience I had last night confirmed it to me. I was sitting in the dark next to Jesus when I felt a presence in the room. It was heavy, and I got the impression it was evil. First it punched me and then shoved me around. It finally went to rest somewhere near Jesus. I asked who or what it was, and Jesus sat up as if he were awake and said, 'I am your god.' That frightened me. Jesus then fell back to the bed and breathed heavily in a snarl." I paused, then said, "I think that we're all in over our heads."

Thompson fidgeted in his chair. I knew he wanted to tear into me again with his bare hands, but Russo's firm grasp pulled him back into the seat. The bishop leaned in my direction and said, "Matthew, I sometimes have felt the same way, but the prophet and I have been able to use him for the good of our universal faith and of the world. And then there are the times when he radiates the goodness that could only come from God."

"I'm not sure that's true. Your plans to unify the religions and control all the nations in the European Union is frightening me as well," I informed them.

"What do you think we should do?" the bishop asked.

"I want you to leave me alone. I don't want to be involved any longer. If you continue to include me then I'm going to go to the media with my information," I threatened.

Thompson's face was turning beat red from his anger at me. He edged to the end of his seat. I knew that in another moment he'd be in my lap tearing my heart out if I didn't do something. I pushed my chair back and said, "Gentlemen, you've heard my proposition. I go to the media on Monday unless I'm totally excluded from all this madness and you place more controls on your power and on his. Whatever he might be."

I had made a bold statement. My mind knew they wouldn't agree to it, but I had to say something and make my point. I had made it and wanted them to leave. Russo rose from his seat first. My lungs drew in a breath expecting that he would destroy me if he could. I was shocked when a smile came across his face.

He said, "Matthew, I can understand your feelings in all this. You know that I've asked some of those same questions myself. Let me think about what you've said, but the real question still has to do with our mutual creation. I'm asking for one last visit. Please see him and tell us what we can do. Can you meet us tomorrow night in his hotel room? No matter what happens to me, Prophet Thompson, or even our relationship with you, I want Jesus well again."

His statements caught me by surprise. I was speechless even as they walked out the door. Just before

Russo exited he turned and asked again, "Can I expect you tomorrow night?" My mouth could barely let the positive answer escape my lips, but I agreed. I felt it would be one last gesture, and from there I would have my freedom from their insanity.

I dropped back into my seat behind the desk and popped open my briefcase, dumped some papers inside it, and snapped it shut. My feet felt heavy stepping along the carpet. My entire body felt drained of energy. Placing my hand on the doorknob, I was turning it when I got this feeling that there was something on the other side of the door. There wasn't a sound or a silhouette on the door's window...it was simply a feeling centered somewhere deep inside me. I had felt it before several times as a child, especially when I prayed. Pausing, I waited and listened intently. It was like a beast was giving me a warning. I heard nothing when I strained my ears again. Then the feeling left me. Deciding it must've been my imagination, I opened my door and exited into the hallway towards the exit, climbed into my car, and drove home.

Beth and I had a quiet dinner. She was still angry that I had gotten involved with Russo and Thompson. I hedged around what had transpired that day until I knew I needed to say something. "Beth, I did see Thompson and Russo again today. Now, before you get angry, let me tell you what I told them."

She was glaring at me. I knew I had only a few seconds to get out my defense. "I told them that I saw physical and spiritual problems with the Messiah and that I did not want to be involved with the project any longer. I let them know that I didn't agree with the direction they were going. Then I said that if they didn't leave me alone and curb their power trips, I was going to the media with what I knew."

"And they walked away without any problem?" she asked incredulously.

"Not exactly," I told her meekly.

She screamed at me, "Not exactly! What does not exactly, exactly mean, Matthew?"

"I agreed to examine him one more time to see if my findings were correct. I'm going tomorrow night and then I'll be done with them," I told her.

She stood and left the room. After dinner I usually cleaned up the kitchen while she relaxed in the bathtub. I was hoping that her time alone would help her understand the situation I was in. My body turned towards the dirty dishes in the sink when the phone rang. The first thought I had was that it was unusually late. I only got calls at that hour when there was a problem at my lab.

My hand snapped the phone from its cradle, and before I could say hello I heard the voice of my friendly C.I.A. director on the phone. "Matthew, how did your meeting go today?"

"How did you know? Are you in town now?"

"No, but one of my agents emailed me an audio tape he made outside your lab. He was using a telescoping microphone to pick up the conversations of your two friends," Hesidence reported.

"So, you know that I told them to stay away from me?" I asked.

"Yes, but I also know something you don't know. Let me play the recording for you." At that point he started the digital recorder.

I heard the booming voice of the prophet attempting a whisper first. "What do we do with MacDonald? He's a loose cannon."

Russo returned, "I agree. If he were to tell someone that the Messiah is ill and is probably dying, then Phase Two of our plan would die with him. That plan is too important. That's why I invited him to the hotel room tomorrow. I wanted to know that he would be around for a few days."

"What are you thinking?" Thompson asked with what sounded like a joyful tone.

"Tonight, my two bodyguards visit the MacDonalds. When it's all over, the police will think that they were killed in a home invasion," Russo answered.

"Why both of them?"

Russo laughed. "Reverend Thompson, he may have told her everything." There were a few moments of silence before Russo continued. "He's also very close to his daughter. We can have her hit while she's here for their funerals. That way we've cleaned up all the loose ends."

Hide me from the secret plots of the wicked...
— *Psalm 64:2*

CHAPTER 19

The recording ended. I was too stunned to say a word, so Hesidence started talking. "Matthew, you have some pretty scary friends, and what's even crazier is that you're protecting them. Tell me what you know and I can work with you."

"What should I do?" I asked.

"Go to the airport and leave town," he answered.

"It would be impossible to get tickets out of here tonight."

"I've already made arrangements. I was having two of my couriers flying back to the States tonight. They'll give up their seats to you. Just go to the counter and see if you can purchase seats. When my couriers see you they'll make the proper arrangements. Now, get out of there. I figure that you have about two hours before your assassins arrive," Hesidence told me.

"Who are the assassins?" I asked.

"You've seen them before. Russo uses his two personal body guards for deeds like this."

"The ones that look like Starsky and Hutch?" I blurted out.

"I never thought of it like that, but yeah, you're absolutely right. Now, be careful, Matthew."

I hung up the phone and ran up the stairs to Beth. Her first reaction when I told her was tears. She cried for fear. She cried because of what I had gotten us into. She cried because we had to leave behind everything we'd collected and bought over the years. She cried to release the tension. Following the tears, Beth flew into action. She packed two bags quickly for herself and me while I went through my home desk to make sure that no names and addresses of our friends in the States were left behind. I planned to drop Beth at my old friend's house.

My old friend, Mary Grace, and I had gone through grade school, middle school, high school, and then to a good Catholic college together. She was more like a sister than anything else. Sometimes the two of us had thought of going off to be a priest and a nun. Of course, Mary Grace was one of the earliest believers in women's rights. She fluctuated between being a nun and a priest. Her frustration over the Catholic Church's restrictions on women may have been one of the reasons why she eventually left the church. More likely, it was because she fell in love with a seminary student named Brian Guthrie.

Brian had started his own church outside of Washington, D.C. in an outlying town called Riverdale. It was a mix of charismatic, evangelical, and Episcopalian. It was simply referred to as The Chapel. The growth had been very surprising to the older staid and traditional churches in the area. Brian's ability with music and his intensely deep understanding and ability to plainly explain the Bible brought thousands of hurting seekers of

God through The Chapel's doors. In Mary Grace, Brian had an excellent partner in a ministry that was reaching into the real lives of people in the D.C. area.

I knew Mary Grace and Brian would both be sympathetic to our problems, and at the same time I was aware that The Chapel was referred to as a dissenting church; more precisely, they weren't followers of the new Messiah and his unification of the world's faiths. We would and could be safe there.

Dissenting churches came in as many different varieties as there were people in churches. Some were fronts for more radical racist groups, others for militias, and some belonged to the broader patriot movement. The Chapel linked itself with no group. It held to a conservative view of the Bible, but wouldn't have been considered a member of the radical religious right. As pastor, Brian Guthrie wanted to give his congregation the Bible's view. He didn't see how the two fit together, and had moved his flock outside of the traditional churches that linked themselves to the clone's unification of the faiths. The Chapel was never seen as a political or armed threat. It was simply people with a dissenting view.

As Beth packed, I worked on a decoy. In the garage I had two large bags of sand, and in the attic was a full-size cut-out of me that Beth had made for my fortieth birthday. I dragged the bags and the cut-out into the bedroom. I bent my oversized photo in half and stuffed part of it under the covers, while the rest of "me" stuck out as if I was sitting up in bed. With the small lamp on the nightstand shining on my life sized photo, it would be hard for anyone peering through the window's sheer curtains to tell what it really was. I hoped anyone peeking would mistake it for me sitting up and working in bed.

Beth walked into the bedroom as I tied rope and twine around the room. "Matthew, what are you doing? We need to get out of here. I'm frightened."

"Beth, if they come soon after we leave and find the lights on but no movement, or the lights off and no movement, they'll break in and discover we've left. If they do it too soon then the assassins might catch us at the airport. This will slow them down," I said as I pointed to my rigging.

"Matt, I don't want to sound stupid, but how?" she asked.

"This bag of sand is heavier than that bag. Just before we leave, I'll poke a hole in it. The sand will slowly come out until the bag hanging in the air becomes the heavier one. When the one in the air falls it will pull this rope attached to the twine. And the twine will pull the chain on the light and then pull over my fortieth birthday gift so it looks like I've laid down. They'll wait until they see the light go out, and then probably hang back for another half hour. That should be enough time for us to be on the airplane," I told her proudly as I pointed to the different elements of my decoy.

"Okay, Mister Bond, I'm ready to leave unless you're planning to have to have a martini, shaken and not stirred, before we go," she joked. It was her attempt at lightening the moment. I appreciated it.

We headed downstairs and into the garage. I slipped out of the side garage door and crept along my neighbor's side of the hedges. I wanted to see if we had any company lying in wait beyond the end of our driveway. I saw nothing, so I pushed open the garage door and slowly backed the car out. Then I secured the door and jumped back in the car. I was ready to back out of the drive when a car tooled down our street. Both of us held our breath. At first I thought it was slowing down. My eyes must've been playing tricks on me, because in another minute it went on by.

I backed out and then gunned the car in the direction of the airport, maneuvering through every rarely used street I could think of. It took us extra time, but I didn't want to be discovered on the road. It would be better to take the longer, "less scenic" route.

Once at the airport, I pulled the car into the parking area, stopping in a no parking zone, and we leaped out. I decided to leave the keys in and the doors unlocked. If it had been the United States, the vehicle would've been stolen and in some chop shop in a few hours—totally untraceable. In Zurich I wasn't as sure, but I hoped airport security would find the car and at least tow it away. That way, the car would not be easily found by our assassins.

We both wanted to run through the terminal to a departing flight gate, but every instinct told me not to draw attention to ourselves. We walked calmly, chatting and keeping our heads down. As we passed the different monitors, I checked for flights to the United States. Swissair had one leaving in thirty-five minutes.

I went to the counter and asked for two tickets. I had been right earlier. There were no tickets available and I saw no one walking up to us. I turned again to the counter to beg for the first possible seats when I was tapped on the shoulder. I looked around to see a thin framed man. He smiled at me, saying, "Excuse me, but I heard you mention a need for two tickets. Our plans were just canceled and we have two seats available."

"Can we make arrangements with the ticket counter then?" I asked.

"Sure, let's talk with these counter people and get you on this plane." In a few minutes, Beth and I were moving slowly down the aisle of the airplane, searching for our seats. We found them and dropped our weary bodies into their soft cushions. It would be a long flight, but both of us would probably sleep for the whole trip.

I started to relax and mentally go through what we had carried with us. Beth had grabbed clothes, photos, and lifetime memorabilia from Cari and her kids. In my backpack were copies of the important clone files and fifteen thumb drives with evidence I had gathered. I had been scanning my notebooks and Russo's diary over the last few months. Digital copies were a lot easier to carry, and certainly lighter than forty boxes of notes.

My family was still in danger. I decided that I wouldn't reveal any of my knowledge and files to the C.I.A. unless I was assured that everyone would be safe. Besides, I wasn't sure that Hesidence had the power to protect us. What if his government decided to jump onto the clone's bandwagon? I'd be eliminated in a minute. Politics was nothing to trust your life to. I knew that I would hold the information. I only wish that I had released it sooner than I am doing right now as I write this.

The jet's engines roared as we taxied down the runway. Any moment we would be safe until our assassins could catch a plane and join us in the United States. I had a several hour head start on the killers, and wanted to put as much distance between us and them as possible.

The pilot revved the engines, and then I noticed a long shadow falling on the carpeted aisle next to me. It moved slowly, stopping at each row as if it were checking or searching for us. The shadow moved closer until, with one of its extremities raised in the air, it got closer and closer to me. I expected any minute to be attacked by my invisible, dark assailant. I closed my eyes. I didn't want to know what was coming next. Suddenly I felt a tap on my shoulder.

"Sir, would you like a pillow for the trip?"

I popped my eyes open and saw the bright smile of the Swissair stewardess. I laughed inside, took the pillow, and was soon out cold from exhaustion.

And this is the condemnation, that the light has come into the world, and men loved darkness rather than light, because their deeds were evil. — John 3:19

CHAPTER 20

Russo pushed the door open quickly when the limo rolled to its stop at the bishop's plush hotel. His two personal body guards leaped to his sides and fell into step.

"Anthony?" Russo said.

"Yes, Your Eminence, how can I be of service?" the dark haired guard said.

Anthony Soteri had grown up on the streets of Chicago. Like Russo, life had been tough and had caused a certain hard edge to both of them. Russo looked for power to control mankind, and Soteri found his power in whacking people. He had been a small time hit man and soldier for the Chicago mob when he bumped into his old friend, Johnny Russo, at the baptism of his sister's little girl.

The two struck up right where they'd left off. That drew the attention of the Family's Don. He knew that Russo was headed for the Vatican, and he wanted to make sure that his investments were watched over. Anthony moved with Russo as his personal aid, but he was rarely seen with the priest in public. It hadn't been until years later that Soteri moved into his role as bodyguard. When he did he brought along a friend—a polish kid named Chuckie Hat.

"I want you two to go right now to Matthew MacDonald's house, and I want that S.O.B. taken out," Russo told them.

"Killed, or beaten and killed?" Chuckie Hat asked. No one really knew Chuckie's real name. Only Soteri and Russo were privy to that information. Actually, most people who got close to Chuckie died. He was a psychotic, full blown and out of the closet. His choice would have been to beat, then beat again before beating again and killing. Everyone else hated the sandy haired snake...everyone except Russo. The bishop had felt a strange kindred spirit when they first met. Anthony was more faithful to the priest, but the Hat could be trusted to get the job done.

"Just killed. I want it to look like a burglary. I don't want to get any questions, but I do want you to bring me a few items."

The three had reached the bishop's room. After Chuckie and Anthony did the hit on MacDonald, he wanted another matter taken care of—a Polish cardinal that stood in his way.

The bishop dropped into an overstuffed leather chair and sucked in a deep breath before speaking. "I want all of his computer storage and all of his hardware. You can leave the monitor, but everything else will most likely have incriminating evidence. I want it done. I want it done now!"

Chuckie leaped from his chair and grinned. He always liked it when he could use his particular gifts and talents on the job site.

An hour later the two of them pulled up in front of the MacDonald house.

"We'll wait until he falls asleep," Anthony said as he lit a cigarette.

"You know those things are going to kill you," Chuckie Hat said.

"If they don't I've got a feeling Russo will. I've known the guy for who knows how many years, but lately there's something really strange going on with the dude. It's like someone else lives inside his body with him. I don't like the vibes I get from that other thing," Soteri rattled.

"Strange. I really like the vibes I get from His Bishopship. I feel energized just being near him. I haven't felt that way since I lived in Florida." The Hat went quiet.

"So what happened in Florida?" Anthony asked, in hopes that his partner's story would help make the time go by faster.

"I used to do these cocaine deals with a guy from the islands down there. Man, what was his name? Goyo. Yeah, that's it. Goyo. Anyway the dude used to play congas for some stupid disco band, but before that he played for the Santeria."

"I never heard of that group. They didn't play the blues, I take it?" Soteri said.

"It ain't a group. It's a religion down there. Kind of a cross between voodoo and Catholic. Anyways, this Goyo took me to a few parties of this bizarre offshoot of the Santeria. They weren't like any church ice cream socials that I went to when I was a kid. These people got down. It was like the whole group would get possessed of the devil and go chasing around all crazy like."

"Did you ever get possessed by the devil at those meetings?" Soteri really wanted to know, but at the same time didn't want to know. After being with Russo he felt an uneasiness around all things devilish. It was something he felt, and a few times he'd even seen something. It wasn't that Hell scared him. If there really was one, Soteri knew he was headed there on a fast train.

"I don't know what it was, but I kind of went into a trance and drank this horrible stuff that I think would have killed me if I wasn't all hopped-up on pot. Then suddenly it was like this roaring lion leaped inside of me and I felt powerful. I mean really powerful. I started tearing chickens apart and eating their guts. After that I don't remember much, although someone told me that we sacrificed a kid and ate it. That part I didn't believe. No matter how hopped up I used to get, I never ate kids."

"I'll remember to keep my sister's kids away from you. Just in case," Anthony said, just before the bedroom light's turned off and caught his eye.

"I don't see him anymore. I guess he went beddy bye," Chuckie joked. "Nighty night. Sleep tight. Don't let the bed bugs bite."

"We go in a half hour," Soteri told his partner as they checked their watches.

The half hour passed and the two slid from their vehicle, then moved quickly and quietly across the street to the house. Anthony cut the wires to the alarm system while Chuckie picked the lock on the back door. He slipped inside with Soteri right behind him.

"Let's get this done and get out of here as fast as we can," the dark haired man said.

"I'd prefer to have a little party with the missus first," Chuckie sneered.

"No time. We can't get caught. Let's do them, grab the stuff, and we're out of here."

"Spoil sport."

"It's a good thing they don't have children or you'd be out back firing up the grill," Anthony whispered.

"C'mon now, a guy eats one little kid and you have him as a psychotic kiddie cannibal."

"If the shoe fits, partner."

They both went silent as they reached the hallway. Soteri motioned for the Hat to climb the stairs first. He slipped up them quietly, using the side portion of the steps to prevent creaking. The Hat reached the top and Soteri ascended them next.

"Which one is their bedroom?" Chuckie mouthed in the pale moonlight.

Anthony pointed straight ahead. He wasn't sure, but they had to start somewhere. Right choice. Pushing the door open slowly, they could see the two bodies sleeping in the bed.

Anthony had started across the room when his foot struck something large and hard. He went tumbling over the sandbag in the middle of the room and crashed to the floor. The Hat thought quickly and leaped over him to the bed. He pumped four shots into each body, but no blood came out. Only feathers fluffed into the air and floated slowly back down.

Chuckie whipped back the sheets.

"Crap! MacDonald is gone! The bishop is not going to like this," the light haired man said.

Soteri pulled himself back to his feet while the Hat flipped on the light. Anthony stared around. "Hey, ya gotta give the guy credit. This is some elaborate setup. This ain't some dumb jerk doctor here. I better call Russo."

The dark haired bodyguard pulled his cell phone from his pocket and punched in the bishop's private number.

"Is it done?" the voice said as it came on the line.

"No, Your Eminence. MacDonald has already split."

"Split?!" There was a long silence before Russo spoke again. "Grab the computer stuff and get back here. No wait…look around and try to find anything that might give you an idea of where he could've gone. Everybody slips up somewhere. Don't let this be where you two slip up." The cell phone went dead.

"We need to search for a clue as to where they went," Soteri said to Chuckie Hat. "You look around up here and I'll check downstairs."

Soteri went into Matthew's study and started packing up the computer equipment, grabbing everything that might have data storage on it. Then he went to the desk and yanked open the drawers, dumping the contents on the floor.

Soteri said to himself, "It looks like you grabbed all your addresses and correspondence, Matty boy. You are starting to gain my respect. Of course, I'll still kill you, but I'll respect you in the morning."

As he was raising up from the last drawer his eye was drawn to a piece of paper caught at the back of the desk. He pulled it out and looked at it just as he felt another presence enter the room.

I will no longer talk much with you, for the ruler of this world is coming — John 14:30

CHAPTER 21

"Find something?" the Hat asked.

"Yeah, but not much. This guy is really good. He grabbed all the correspondence and most of the computer storage, but this little bit of information was caught behind a drawer. It says, 'Professor Grant, Bio-geneticist, 4712 2nd Street, Philadelphia.' I'd bet that he's going to see this guy."

"Why?"

"Burglar's intuition. Did you find anything?" Soteri asked.

"Nah, but I did grab this picture of the two. It looks recent. It'll help somewhere down the line."

The two grabbed the boxes of computer hardware and software, carried them to the car, and were gone.

***

"Beth, wake up," I said to my resting wife.

"Why? Are we there?" she responded groggily.

"No, but I had a thought. Hesidence wanted us to take these two tickets so his men could meet us at the other end. We can't take that risk. The government could turn to the Messiah's side at any time, and then our gooses are cooked."

"Geese."

"What?"

"The plural of goose is geese. You're a Nobel Prize winner; I think you should know that."

I stared at my wife and then smiled.

"Go ahead, dear," she said, "I agree with you, but how do we dodge them on the other end?"

I pulled my carry-on bag from the seat in front of me, then unzipped it and showed her the contents.

"My wigs and a hat. I don't get it," she said with a look of confusion on her face.

"As we land we pull on the wigs and you put the hat on. That guy two rows in front of you has hit on every stewardess and woman near him. As you leave start a conversation with him. Flirt a little bit. He'll be very attentive, and most people will think that you're with him. That will get you out of here."

"And you?" she asked.

"They'll be looking for a man and a woman together. The wig and limp should work," I answered.

"Then what?"

"Meet me at Avis. We'll rent a car and get out of there. Just remember that we need to talk about our trip to Maine," I told her.

"Maine?" Beth said with a startled voice. "I thought we were going to Washington, D.C.?"

"We are, but the conversation will throw off anyone following us. Now, get some more sleep. We'll need to be rested when we get there." I wished I could have slept, but instead my nodding off was only filled with nightmares. Nightmares of us being caught somewhere between Hesidence's CIA and Russo's assassins.

I'd finally fallen into a fitful sleep when suddenly there was a tap on my shoulder. "Sir, we'll be landing soon. You'll need to put your seat upright and fasten your seat belt."

I rubbed my face hard to get the circulation going in an attempt to wake up faster; our disguises had to be prepared. It was my hope that this idea would buy us the time we needed. My plan had been to see my old professor, Samuel Grant. But after Hesidence played the tape of the assassins in our house, in my rush to get out I didn't realize till later that I had left Grant's address in the desk. I wanted Grant to help me dig for the answer to the Messiah's genetic degradation. It could be useful information when the time came to save our lives. It was wishful thinking.

Beth awakened. "Are we there yet?"

"Remember, dear, as we all stand up to leave put the wig and hat on. Then—"

"I know, flirt with the big mouth Romeo over there. I don't know if I can remember how to flirt," Beth said.

"Don't worry. Anytime a beautiful woman says anything to a guy like that his player mode takes over."

We were descending. The lights of New York City stretched out like a glimmering, rolling sea. Touchdown came.

The other passengers scurried to their feet and busied themselves getting their luggage. It was the perfect time for Beth and I to slip into our alter-egos. I felt a little like Superman changing into another identity in hopes of saving the world. Beth popped on her wig and hat, then added her reading glasses. It was a nice touch since they were tinted and would keep anyone from seeing her distinctive eye color.

Beth moved quickly, weaving and wiggling through the crowd of people until she ended up next to her mark. She spoke to him and the guy responded exactly as I had predicted. The flow of passengers pushed towards the door on their way out.

I watched as Beth and her companion walked through the gate and out into the aisle heading for the luggage. Beth and I hadn't checked anything. All we had was in the bags we carried. I felt it was better to get away with our lives than with the many memories we had to leave behind.

Out of the corner of my eye I noticed two men in dark suits who were very officious looking. It made me believe that these two were members of my reception committee. Their eyes shifted from one passenger to another. I moved an extra few people between us by sidestepping in the flow of humans greeting old friends and family. Soon my back was to the men and I was hustling towards the car rental booth near the baggage claim.

I glanced back once after I was about one hundred feet away. The two men were moving in a frantic manner. They knew they had lost us, and I was certain they would be checking the faces around them more closely. Up ahead was an opening. Obviously, it was area under construction. The lights were out and a strip of yellow plastic ribbon stretched across the entrance. It headed in the same direction as I was going, but it had the wonderful security of darkness. I had to make it there before the CIA agents saw me.

Everyone from our flight was hurrying to the baggage area when they came into contact with a group from another flight. Dozens more bodies merged in with ours. No one would notice one figure slipping out of the stream and into a dark corridor. I saw my opportunity and took it.

Inside the dark hall, I was able to make out the lights at the other end. I was smiling to myself about my successful avoidance of the CIA while listening to my steps reverberating in the hallway. For a moment I felt peaceful until I heard it. It was unmistakable….it was the heavy breathing of an animal.

***

About the same time that Beth and I were racing through the Kennedy Airport, our would-be assassins had made it back to Rome. Through other sources I was told the general flow of conversation in the Vatican at that hour.

"Your Eminence," Soteri said.

"Come here, Anthony and Charles. Tell me the bad news." Russo dropped into the large, overstuffed chair behind his oversized mahogany desk. "How did you let them slip out of your hands, and what did you find? Then tell me where they went."

"Can't," Chuckie responded.

"Can't what?" the bishop snapped.

"Don't know anything yet," Hat said.

Russo leaped to his feet and grabbed a small statue. It was a priceless Renaissance piece, but that didn't stop Russo from flinging it across the room into a bookcase of ancient manuscripts. It crashed against the brittle spines of the books, sending both clay fragments and particles of old, frail paper exploding into the air.

"I can't believe that you let him slip away," the bishop screamed with an intensity that shocked both men.

"We didn't. Somebody must've tipped him off. By the time we arrived his place was deserted. Who else did you talk to about this?" Anthony asked.

"No one. After Thompson and I discussed it, I talked to you two. Only four of us knew what was going to happen. I never said a word to anyone. You say that you didn't slip up. That leaves only one person. Even he is becoming a bit of a problem."

"I'll whack him for ya, Bishop Russo," the Hat spit out.

"I don't want either of you to 'do' him. I just want MacDonald and his wife eliminated. Now get back there and find out where they went for sure. Try the airport. Show their pictures around. If that doesn't work check the other ticket counters around the city. I want him struck down before he strikes down our operation here."

Soteri nudged Chuckie Hat and the two turned and exited. Russo stood up from his soft chair, but wobbled as if he were faint. His body jerked, throwing him back in his chair, and then he went limp. Instantly after collapsing, the bishop's body leaped from the seat and swiped his arm along the top of his desk, pushing papers, the phone, pens, and photos onto the floor.

Then he spoke. It was his voice, but there was something very different about it.

"MacDonald, I see you. I know where you are. You will not defeat my plan. You will not defeat me. I am the ruler of this earth. The ruler of this planet. It is mine. Your ancestor gave it to me, and I'm not about to surrender it. I'll end your life and the lives of everyone around you. I see you now. You should not have gone into the darkness. The darkness is mine. I love darkness, and in the darkness men do evil deeds. Now, you are mine."

162

Be sober, be vigilant; because your adversary the devil walks about like a roaring lion, seeking whom he may devour. — I Peter 5:8

CHAPTER 22

I could feel the presence of someone or something with me in the hallway. My heart beat fast as it crept into my throat and then to my parched mouth. The sweat on my palms made it difficult to hold onto my bag. What was it? What was with me? I quickened my pace.

Suddenly, as if I were an inflatable doll, I was tossed to the side, smashing hard and heavily into the wall. My body made a heavy thud that reverberated in the empty hall. As I slid to the floor, fear raced through me and gripped my mind.

"Who is it? What do you want?" I cried out.

Again I was lifted and then rammed into the wall on the other side of the hall. My suitcase went sailing down the waxed floor toward the light at the other end. Fortunately, I had placed all my data, research, Russo's diary copy, and dozens of thumb drives in my back pack that was secured to my body.

I scrambled to my feet and ran towards the light at the end of the hall. The presence kept pace right behind me. I could feel its hot breath getting closer and closer to the back of my neck. Fear crept through my mind as a strange smell like rotten eggs wafted around my face. I knew the smell but didn't want to believe it. I could smell sulfur.

I ran by my suitcase and had bent to scoop it up when the piece of luggage leaped into the air and slammed into my rib cage. The air in my lungs was forced from my body in a loud gasp while I stumbled over my own feet. I kept my balance, but with each step my knees grew wobbly and weak, like the gravity beneath me was continually increasing its pull.

Without warning I saw a murky form move onto me and felt a heavy weight on my chest, and then something like thin bones wrapped around my throat. I hadn't caught my breath since the flying suitcase, and now the remainder of it was being choked out of my body. What was this? What was happening to me?

My mind started to cloud like a dark shroud was being pulled over my head. For some reason the word shroud popped into my mind, and with that the image of the crucified Christ that had been imprinted on it. In the vision the nail pierced hands were free of the cloth and they reached toward me.

"Jesus," I choked out, just before I felt a rush of wind and heard the sound of colliding bodies. I couldn't see anything, but the sound was unmistakable. I had heard it many times during my college football days when two linemen charged each other, coming together in a powerful thump. As soon as I heard the colliding bodies the weight lifted off me and the choking fingers untangled from around my throat.

I lay on my back, sucking in fresh air. I wanted to stay there. My exhausted, aching body needed rest and my empirical mind needed to figure out what had happened, but the intense fear that still raced through my body forced me to my feet. I grabbed my suitcase and ran down the hall. It wasn't until I reached the end that I stopped to take stock of my appearance.

My hat and wig had fallen off somewhere in the hall, and I wasn't about to go back for them. I brushed my fingers through my red hair, trying to straighten it the best I could. It was then that I felt the bruises that must have lined my body. I wasn't sure, but I had a feeling that at least one rib was broken.

What had happened? What had attacked me? I had a feeling I knew, but didn't want to think about. Instead, I needed to get to my wife at the car rental booth.

The field is the world, the good seeds are the sons of the kingdom, but the tares are the sons of the wicked one. The enemy who sowed them is the devil, the harvest is the end of the age — Matthew 13:38-39

CHAPTER 23

I looked down the hallway and saw the sign for the Avis Rental. Beth was near it, but not close enough that we would be seen together. I approached the counter and started the paperwork procedure for the rental. I purposely used my charge card. I wanted to leave a trail right to the counter clerk.

"It looks like a beautiful day for a drive," I told her.

"Yes, Mr. MacDonald. What's your destination?" she asked.

"I'm heading to Maine for a few days, and then back to here to catch a flight to Florida," I said.

"Like you said, it is certainly a good day for a drive," she said as her fingers dropped the keys to a foreign four door sedan into my hands. I headed to the shuttle bus that would carry me to the rental car lot.

Beth was only a few feet behind me, acting as if we didn't know each other. I turned and spoke loud enough for the clerk to hear, "It should be a nice ride to Maine, hon." It was time for Beth to be seen with me. If my wife was not at my side when I exited the airport it would cause Starsky and Hutch or my friend from the C.I.A. to ask too many questions.

As we went through the doors Beth spun me around.

"What happened to you?" she asked with a worried and frightened voice.

"I don't know, Beth. I never saw what attacked me. I smelled it. I felt it. I heard it, but I never saw it. The encounter made me sure of one thing: I'm doing the right thing. As soon as I figure out what happened to me, I'll tell you."

***

Our daughter Cari had started her departure moments after I called. She grabbed her children's clothes and threw them in a large suitcase along with her own clothes. In her haste she made one mistake. Cari picked up the phone and called her best friend, Jeanna Bashara. Jeanna and Cari were both single mothers, and often shared the struggle of raising children on their own. Jeanna worked as a secretary at St. Joseph the Worker Catholic Church a few miles from Cari's home.

From what Cari told me their conversation went like this.

"Hi, Jeanna. I can't explain right now but I have to leave town immediately. There's a family emergency."

"What is it?"

"I can't say, but please stop by my house later today and grab my cat and plants. I'll call you in a few days and let you know what happened."

"Cari, you're scaring me."

"Jeanna, everything will be all right. I'll be fine and the kids will be fine. Before you know it, we'll be back. But to be real honest, I don't know what's going on. It scares me a little as well, but my dad sounded desperate and very emphatic that I meet him immediately."

"Where are you meeting him?"

"Jeanna, I can't tell you, but I'll call when I get there. Take care, and kiss your kids for me." She was out the door and in her car heading for Riverdale to meet us.

***

Beth and I climbed into our rental car and drove out of the airport. I had hoped that the rental counter clerk would remember Maine as our destination and send our pursuers off in the opposite direction. Beth and I pushed along the highway hoping to avoid getting stopped or involved in any type of accident. I wanted to leave no trail from New York to Washington, D.C. I had already pitched our cell phones, and planned to pick up some pre-pays along the route. In a way, I thought it was ironic that I'd be hiding out less than an hour from Hesidence's office.

We made it to Mary Grace's house about mid-morning. When I rounded the corner and rode up over the hill, my old friend was standing in her front yard overlooking the flower beds that flowed beneath the bay windows. She always grew flowers because of her son, Trevor. Trev would often appear through the kitchen door with different colored pollens dusting his upper lip and around his nostrils. But that was all part of a time more pleasant and more settled.

She heard our car pull up and twisted around. Her mouth went wide open with surprise. "Matthew! Beth! What in the world are you doing here?"

"It's a long story," I answered as I wearily crawled from behind the wheel of the car and went into a full body stretch.

169

"Good. Brian is home and we'll all sit and have a cup of coffee, and you can tell us this mysterious long story of yours," she told me as she hugged Beth and I.

For hours I explained our situation and showed them different items that I had brought along. When I got to the part about the airport's dark hallway, I tried my best to tell the others what I thought it was. It was then that Brian finally spoke up.

"Matthew, I really think that you're in the middle of a battle that is a lot bigger than any of us. The scripture says that we wrestle with powers that we know little about," he said.

Beth leaned forward and sat at the end of the couch. "What do you mean?"

"I believe that Matthew is a part of a great battle between good and evil. Things are happening in the spiritual realm that he is intimately involved with. You see, the Bible is plain that there are 'principalities and powers' that rule this earth. They're not earthly, but spiritual powers. These are things he doesn't know anything about, but at the same time he seems to have all the information at his fingertips to thwart the evil one's plans," Brian said with a somber tone.

"But what is it that I have?" I asked.

"I'm afraid that only you can figure that out. My fear is that if you don't do it soon, then the whole world will be caught in the greatest battle of all times. Matthew, you've come face to face with Satan and his Antichrist. The problem is that there are only a few of us who would believe you, and I have a feeling that believing you will cost people their lives."

The room went silent. We were afraid to look at Brian. What if he was right?

I cleared my throat and spoke. "What are my choices?"

"Figure it out and you may save the world," Brian answered, then continued, "or you can sit on what you know and hope that you're never found. Maybe by doing that you can protect yourself and your loved ones."

"What about you, Brian? What would you do?" Beth asked.

"I'm going to meet several of the other dissenting pastors and get out the information that Matthew can give me. I'm afraid that I signed on to do battle with the devil a long time ago. Before it was just one soul at a time. Now, it looks like the odds have increased," Brian answered.

"I can't give you anything, Brian. My fear is that it could get you all killed," I said.

"'To live is Christ. To die is gain.' Those are the words of the Apostle Paul, and I guess we've got to take our chances," Mary Grace added. She and Brian took each other's hand, and I could see them squeeze hard. They had made their commitment.

"I've got to go to Philadelphia tomorrow to see an old professor of mine. He should help me answer some of those questions. After that I'll come back here and we'll make copies of everything for you. I think you're taking a big risk though," I told my friend's husband.

"I don't. I've been given a holy trust. If I was a Presbyterian I'd say that God foreordained for you to come walking in my door. And even if I'm not a Presbyterian I believe that anyway," he answered.

I could feel my body finally relax. I needed sleep and I needed it badly. Brian and Mary Grace showed us to their guest room. Within moments of me slipping under the covers I was asleep.

For truly, when we were with you, we told you before that we should suffer tribulation; even as it came to pass, and you know. — I Thessalonians 3:4

CHAPTER 24

Thompson was ushered into Bishop Russo's chambers. "Have you heard anything?"

"No, but I have a strong feeling they are already in the United States. Most likely in New York, but where they went from there I don't know. The guy tossed his cell phone so I can't even get a GPS trace on it. If he releases any of his information, then our plans are ruined. We need to hurry into phase two now."

"I'm already on it. I've got Laura, Reverend Jack Ripton, and a friend of mine that's in the CIA ready to leave for Israel," Thompson reported.

"Send them, now!" Russo seethed as the command left his lips.

***

Laura, Ripton, and Agent Joshua Longtree exited the doors of the airplane in Tel Aviv. They were on a mission. Very few knew the real purpose. Very few would ever know what they were really doing there.

Longtree was a former congregation member of the Prophet Thomas Thompson. Over the years, the prophet had gained more and more of a hold over the agent's mind. Not by some kind of brainwashing, but with a little old-fashioned blackmail. Joshua hid a few secrets that would end his career, and one of them would even put him in prison. Joshua Longtree had been entrapped by a foreign agent into giving highly sensitive secrets to an unfriendly government.

Joshua was stuck, and Thompson had been able to eliminate the foreign agent. For that action Longtree was forever grateful. All Thompson wanted was a favor every once in a while, and now it was time once again to pay the piper.

Walking next to Longtree was Jack Ripton, the second most popular televangelist on the airwaves. What Ripton lacked in supernatural power he made up for in pure deceit. His charismatic smile won the hearts of millions, and millions in cash came to him every day of the week.

The interesting thing about Ripton was that he'd gotten into TV preaching because he thought there could be a lot of money in it. He could never be construed as a religious or even spiritual man. He often joked with one of his old college mates that he could be the best televangelist on the screen. Then he'd go into his fake voice, made up unknown tongue, and irritating squinting. Years later they became the tools of his trade. He and Thompson were made for each other.

Once in Tel Aviv, Ripton departed for his meetings with government officials. His goal was to set up a globally televised Good Friday sermon by Jesus from Golgotha, the spot where the real Christ had been crucified. The Israeli government was excited to be a part of it. They needed some good press after the Mideast problems of late.

The Jewish people had not totally signed on to the fact that this may be their Messiah, but more and more were seeing the great similarities. As a symbol of their belief in his striving for world peace, they planned to place a statue of him somewhere on the grounds of where the original temple had stood. The clone was excited about it and couldn't wait for the details to be worked out. He wanted to have the worship of his own people, the Children of Israel. It was very important to him.

Laura went with Longtree. Their mission was a little more quiet. In fact, only one man would know what they wanted. Joshua had worked with David Abraham before. He was one of those people who would do anything for the right price. The kind of person that Russo and Thompson liked.

Laura stood in the shade of a tree as the two men sat talking only a few feet away.

"Do you understand what I want you to do?" Longtree quizzed.

"I gotta pop the Christ guy. It won't be that hard," David answered.

"That is only part of it. It must be done with a single bullet between the eyes and while he is speaking to millions of people on television," Joshua summed it up again.

"Listen, the price is right. A million dollars is hard to turn down, but it won't do me any good when I'm caught. The police will kill me, or the courts will try me and kill me. Either way, dead men don't get to spend much money," Abraham said.

"That's where I come in. I'll be near you. Once your shot has done its work, then I'll pull out my gun and shoot you—"

"Wait a second...no matter what I still end up dead," David butted in.

"Give me a chance to explain. My shot will be a blank. You fall down, break the bag of fake blood, and swallow this capsule. It will make it appear, even to the best of doctors, that you are dead. That night, your family, guided by me, will pick up your body. Hours later you come back to life and I sneak you out of the country to the United States. There you can spend your million dollars in a very lively way."

"Are you sure this plan will work?" Abraham asked.

"Positive."

"Count me in, but I want half up front."

***

I rose the next morning and started my drive to Professor Grant's at 4712 2nd Street, Philadelphia. Grant was the one man who had always been my advisor, and the one man who knew more about cloning than me. I was hoping that Grant could help me discover what was causing the clone of Jesus to deteriorate.

I parked the rental car outside of the downtown area and grabbed a bus into town towards Grant's. I was sure that there would be people looking for the vehicle by now. I couldn't risk being discovered.

Grant's old brownstone apartment building looked the same as it had so many years ago when I would come and talk about my doctoral thesis. It showed the years of painted-over, peeling paint that was painted over again just to peel again and to be painted over again. The stone stairs were more worn from the years of tenants and students climbing them.

I pushed the button to ring Grant's apartment.

"Yes, who is it?" the tinny sounding speaker blasted out with Grant's voice.

"Doc, you're not going to believe this, but it's Matthew MacDonald and—"

"Oh my goodness, come in, come in!"

The buzzer rang and the front door's lock was released, and I bounded up the stairs to Grant's apartment. My old mentor was already standing at the open door with his arms open wide and a cane leaning against his leg.

"Matthew, what are you doing here?"

"It's a real long story. Could I buy you dinner and talk about it?"

"Sure, sure. My favorite little cafe is still open around the block. We'll just scoot on over there for some excellent Philadelphia food." The old man scooped up his cane and turned to walk inside. "Let me get my coat and we'll be on our way."

It was then that I asked about the cane. "What's with the cane, Doc?"

"I fell on the ice a few months back and it hasn't been right since. I guess my tap dancing career is over." The professor chuckled at his own joke.

We walked slowly along the old street that I remembered so well as he caught me up on some of my old classmates. We got to the front of the cafe and I held the door open for him. Once inside we sat down at a table where both of us could see the front door. I liked it like that. I was still uncertain whether my trail would be discovered.

"Tell me your story, boy; tell me," he asked.

"My life is in danger," I stammered out.

He laughed at first, then took a serious look at my eyes. "You believe that, don't you?"

"I know it."

"Explain it to me."

We ordered our dinners and ate as I talked all about the cloning and the recent genetic deterioration. It wasn't until I hit the part about the CIA and the two men who were out to kill me that he started to show some signs of doubt.

"Matthew, maybe you've been overworking yourself lately. You're starting to sound a little delusional. It used to happen to me when I was under a lot of stress. A good rest ought to clear this up," Grant said.

"You don't believe me?"

"Some parts are believable, but not this paranoid stuff about being attacked by something you couldn't see in a dark hallway in an airport. Then two men dressed as priests who look like old TV characters that are out to kill you is a little hard to believe," he said with a fatherly, nearly patronizing smile.

"Yeah, I know." I decided not to press the point. What I really wanted from him was his thoughts on the genetic deterioration. "Anyway, I need you to tell me why the clone is starting to die."

"There is no sign of disease?"

"No."

"Then we can surmise that it is something that has been locked inside of his genetic coding. He is suppose to die at...how old did you say he was?" Doc asked.

"Thirty-three."

"Hmm, that's interesting," he said as he rubbed his rough, wrinkled hand over his stubbly chin.

"What is?" I asked with excitement.

"If this is truly a clone of the Messiah, then wasn't Christ crucified around the age of thirty-three?" Grant asked.

"Yeah, but what does that have to do with this?"

"Well—"

Grant's answer was interrupted by the opening of the front door to the cafe. Both of our eyes snapped to the two priests walking in from the cold night. One was dark haired and the other blond. If I had to describe them, I would say they looked like Starsky and Hutch.

Grant's mouth dropped open until his chin nearly rested on his chest. He turned his eyes to me and his face away from the two and spoke very softly. "Holy Mary, Mother of God, you weren't delusional. Please, forgive me."

"You're forgiven, but what do I do now? Is there a back door out of here?" I asked with trembling lips.

"Just sit tight, Matthew. I have an idea." As the waiter walked by Grant called him over and talked softly to the young man. "What's that flaming thing you make with the sherry and rum?"

"That is an appetizer, sir. Not a dessert," the waiter said, as if he was talking to a confused old man.

"I know that, boy. But my friend and I are devout Catholics, and we want to show our respect for the two priests who just came in. Could you bring that to them on us?" Grant said.

"Why, of course, sir," the waiter said with a big smile, and went into the kitchen.

179

"Kids nowadays; no respect for us old geezers." He said it a little louder than we were previously talking, then went to a whisper again. "When he brings that thing out here I will hook his leg with my cane. The appetizer will go flying towards our two men of the cloth. Hopefully, it will catch their killing butts on fire, but nevertheless it will give you time to race out the back door. Once you're out there turn right and then left. Any other way will lead to a dead end. That way you'll end up right in front of my apartment building. You can grab your bags and go down the back staircase and out that door. With a little luck you'll be far enough away that they won't be able to catch you."

"Thanks, Doc, but be careful," I said with a slight smile.

A moment later the waiter exited the kitchen door with a plate of flames. Soon after he passed us Doc Grant raised his cane and snaked it out, hooking the leg of the young man. The last thing I saw was the air filled with tongues of fire. I could hear screams of pain as I darted through the kitchen, then a gun shot. Then another one echoed behind the first and struck the wall above my head. A third shot popped, but I was already too far away for it to be a bullet designed for me.

Only a newspaper account could fill in what happened next. The two fake priests leaped to their feet and fell back as the flames caught their coats on fire. Soteri was patting himself frantically since most of the flaming liquor had hit him. It was the Chuckie Hat that had pulled his gun.

The first shot hit the poor waiter on the floor as he struggled to his feet. Fortunately, it didn't kill him and left a witness to the scene. The third shot was aimed at

Professor Grant as he hobbled towards them swinging his cane. The shot went through his brain. If they only knew what a wonderful mind they had stopped before I could get the answers that might have saved the clone's life. The answers died with Grant.

Grant was right. I was able to quickly get far enough away that I wasn't followed. His back staircase led to an alley that dumped onto a busy street. I stuck out my thumb, and amazingly the first truck rolling past me stopped.

As I climbed into his cab he asked, "Where ya headin', Red?"

"Wherever you're going."

"I going to head west on the turnpike," he added.

"Will that put me anywhere near New Castle, Pennsylvania?" I asked.

"Sure will. I'll have ya there in about eight hours. Relax, Red. Ya like gospel music?" he asked.

"Some of it," I said.

"Never liked it much myself, but ever since that Jesus clone came on the scene I've been feelin' a whole lot more religious. Say, what'ya think of him, Red?"

"He scares me. He scares me real bad," I mumbled.

I sank down in the seat and listened to the music. It was some kind of country gospel by a group called Daniel Amos. Good stuff, and it kept my friend, the truck driver, from talking too much. I was glad to listen to it on the way to New Castle.

If the world hate you, you know that it hated me before it hated you. — John 15:18

CHAPTER 25

"This is a very important journey, Jesus," Prophet Thompson said to the cloned Messiah. "With this sweep through the Holy Land at Easter time you will have the world's eyes on you. It is imperative that we communicate the right message to your waiting worshipers."

"Yes, yes. You're right, Thomas. I need to — ahh — have you seen my suitcase? I thought I left it in here," the Messiah asked with a confused and weak voice. His confusion was spreading. The bouts with his disease grew stronger every day, and the Messiah's ability to focus dwindled in direct proportion.

Thompson watched him. He shook his head in disbelief as Jesus left the bedroom of his home near Rome.

"It's getting worse, isn't it?" Laura, Thompson's long time secretary and my secret advisor, asked.

"That's all right. We just need to keep him off to himself until the big sermon on Good Friday. After that things will be fine again," the prophet answered.

"I don't see how assassinating your creation is going to make it all better," Laura whispered.

"Laura, please don't mention anything about that ever again. You'll see that it is truly in God's plan."

"Which god are we talking about? The little one on the throne in the Vatican, the one I'm standing next to, or the one who rules over hell?" Laura retorted.

Who is she talking to? How dare her? Smite her! Strike her down!

The voice drove into the prophet's mind and his eyes flashed and his left arm snapped hard in her direction, catching the woman along the bridge of her nose with the back of his hand. Laura flew backwards, crashing into the small writing table and chairs sitting around it. She landed hard, pulling on the table and tipping it forward. Laura slid off and the edge of the table came down painfully on her chest, pushing the air out of her lungs. No scream escaped her lips, but a thin stream of crimson began its trickle down her chin.

"What's all the noise in there?" Jesus yelled from the other room.

"Nothing. Laura just tripped. Just stay there and I'll be in to help you find your suitcase." Thompson looked at her with demon eyes and spat out, "Just keep your mouth shut, you little—"

"Prophet Thompson, what should I wear for the Good Friday sermon?" Jesus said as he stood at the door to the bedroom. He stared down at Laura and remarked, "That was some nasty trip, Laura. Any broken bones that I can heal? You know, I heal people. I'm the Messiah. Messiah's heal people. Do you need me to heal you?"

Thompson made it to Jesus in a few large bounding steps and spun his body around and out the door. The clone's recent drivel was more disconcerting each time Thompson heard him speak.

"She'll be fine. Won't you, Laura?" Thompson called back to her as he left the room.

Laura's hand went to her mouth and wiped away the blood. Over the years Thompson's internal voice, that gave him the gift of prophecy, had changed. It had become more violent in its instructions, and more cruel in how it led the man she had once loved and once respected. Now beatings were more of the norm than the abnormal. Even his interest in sex had moved towards the more perverted. It seemed to her that the prophet had become more twisted inside his heart, brain, and soul. Something was changing him daily, and each day it became more horrible to watch.

She tried to remember back to that hard working Florida pastor in his tiny rural church. He had been so caring to the people he'd called his flock. It was the voice inside his head that had changed him. First it seemed like great miracles would emanate from him. The voice would speak to Thompson and he would speak the future. She was sure that the voice was now guiding his every move. The voice that she had once thought belonged to the Holy Spirit she now felt belonged to all that was unholy.

But Laura was too afraid to run. Running meant her death. Just like what I was facing. Thompson would hunt her down and joyfully choke the life out of her. The beatings were easier to endure than the thought of her death.

**

My friend Mary Grace was truly taking good care of my wife, daughter, and grandchildren. Beth told me later that the two of them had worked out several escape routes in case either the assassins or the CIA showed up. Their plans would come in handy later on.

I didn't expect anyone to find them there, but I didn't expect my daughter to be the one to leave the trail to them either. The morning after arriving at Brian and Mary Grace's, she called her friend, the secretary of St. Joseph the Worker Church. Jeanna had gone over and picked up her cat and plants, and was planning to take care of them.

"Jeanna. Hi, it's me," Cari said from a pay phone around the corner from Mary Grace's home.

"Mystery girl, what's going on?" the secretary said back to her.

"I'm not sure. I got here after Dad fell asleep, and he was gone when I got up. Mom said that our lives are in danger," Cari answered.

"That's kind of hard to believe, isn't it?" Jeanna said.

"Guess who is supposed to be after us?"

"Got me, girl. You're the one with a nutcase for a dad," Jeanna joked.

"Mom said that the Messiah and Archbishop Russo are behind this. Can you imagine that? Jesus and the next pope are trying to kill my father. I'll wait around till Dad gets back and try to convince him to see a doctor and take a long rest. I should be back in a few days," Cari said.

"How can I get hold of you?" Jeanna asked.

"I don't want Dad to know that I talked to anyone, so I'll just sneak out every day and call you. Watch Puffles for me, and don't forget to water those plants. See you soon." Cari hung up and headed back to the house.

As Jeanna was hanging up her phone the door to the church office opened, and in walked two priests. She didn't recognize either one, except that they reminded her of two guys from an old cop show she had seen on TV.

"Hi, can I help you?" she asked.

"Actually, you can help us, the archbishop, and the Messiah, but more importantly you can help a very ill man," Soteri said with a large smile and serious eyes.

"How?"

"You have a friend. Her name is Cari, and her dad is the bio-geneticist that cloned Jesus."

"Yes, that's right."

"Dr. MacDonald has been under severe stress and was under strict medical care. I believe they have diagnosed him with an inoperable tumor. The tumor is giving him paranoid delusions. Archbishop Russo is terribly concerned about one of his oldest and dearest friends, and has sent us to find him. We thought Cari might know where he is, but the neighbors said she left yesterday with luggage and the kids. A very dear old woman, Mrs. Krauser, told us that you came later and picked up the cat," Soteri told her.

"Oh my goodness. I just got off the phone with Cari. She doesn't know about the tumor, but she's also very worried about her dad," Jeanna said with a tone of concern rising in her voice.

"Can you tell us where she is?" Chuckie Hat snapped.

"She wouldn't tell me, but she said she would call again tomorrow."

"From where?" Hat asked.

"She was going to call from a pay phone," Jeanna said, then continued. "I don't know where she called from, but my caller ID has the number recorded. See." She pointed at the small caller ID screen.

"D.C." Hat said to Soteri as he jotted down the number.

"You've been very helpful. We'll track them down, but do us a favor. Don't say a word to her. I don't want the girl frightened about her dad's health. We'll be there tomorrow and make sure he gets the medical care he needs," Soteri said.

The two priests turned and walked out. Jeanna fell back in her chair and let out a long breath of air. This was weighty stuff, and far more than a church secretary could handle.

***

A phone call came in to Russo's private and direct line. The archbishop asked, "Have you found MacDonald yet?" Soteri could hear the intensity in Russo's voice. He had said once to one of my secret information suppliers that he had noticed a new stressfulness on Russo's face and in his voice. The muscles often pulled hard around the jaw. The fake priest couldn't quite put his finger on the way the archbishop looked and acted. Soteri had never seen it before, and with his contacts in organized crime, he thought he had seen it all. I should add that the rumor was that Soteri's past life was a kill or be killed existence. He knew who to fear and who to quietly remove from the ranks of the breathing. Russo was someone to fear. Anthony also knew that the archbishop was quite irritated that I had escaped them again.

"He's covering his tracks well." Soteri spoke rather timidly. Probably, he wasn't quite sure how the soon-to-be Vicar of Christ would take that. "I found out where his daughter is and I think he may be there too. Beyond that, we don't have much to go on now. If we don't catch up to him in D.C., then I think that we should stay somewhere in the U.S. and wait, so if someone sees him, we can get there quickly."

The bishop frowned and said, "There's one more thing you need to do. By letter, contact every priest or nun that MacDonald had as a teacher or pastor. Add a current picture. Tell them to contact the bishop of their diocese if MacDonald shows up. Then contact every diocese with his picture. Let them know that we suspect he joined with a radical underground militia that's plotting to destroy Jesus, and that we want to be notified immediately of any communication they have with him. Now, move on this. I want that letter out today." Russo hung the phone up quickly.

Soteri and Chuckie Hat checked on the phone number they had gotten from Jeanna's caller ID. It belonged to a pay phone in Washington, D.C., but that gave them no clues as to Cari's exact location.

"Doesn't tell us enough, does it?" Hat asked.

"It will be enough. We go to the phone's location, and tomorrow when little Cari comes to make her phone call we'll just follow her back to the good Doctor MacDonald," Soteri answered as he slipped into the car and strapped on his seat belt for the ride to the nation's capital.

The two were in place early the next day and waiting. It wasn't too long before a woman who strongly resembled Cari MacDonald came strolling to the public phone.

"That's her!" Hat said.

"Look at the chick. She is glancing around like this is some kind of spy novel. Don't worry, honey, the mean old bad guys will take care of you quickly," Soteri said.

They waited. Her conversation lasted about five minutes, and then she turned and headed back the way she had come. Soteri eased the car out of his parking space the moment she rounded the corner. He coasted to a halt at the stop sign, and they watched her go down the street two blocks and turn left into a driveway.

Soteri raced the car within a few feet of the driveway and stopped.

"Call Thompson. See if 1147 Cedar Ridge Drive means anything to him."

Chuckie Hat pulled his cell phone from his pocket and punched in the numbers.

"Thompson," the voice on the other end answered. "Who's this?"

"The Hat, Rev," Chuckie answered.

"Did you find him?" Thompson said excitedly.

"We trailed his daughter back to 1147 Cedar Ridge Drive in Riverdale, Maryland. Does the address mean anything to you?" Chuckie asked.

"I'll check. Give me a minute." There was a minute of silence till Prophet Thompson came back on the line. "Well, I think you boys struck pay dirt. That is the home of a pastor from one of the dissenting church groups. What's even more interesting is that only yesterday we had the report that new information that could be damaging to us emanated from there. Oh, and there's more. The pastor's wife was a long-time friend of Matthew MacDonald. I even met her at one of our receptions in D.C. years ago. This will be great. You can eliminate MacDonald, his family, and this pain-in-the-butt pastor's family all at one time. I'm telling you, boys, it don't get any better than this. Nice work. Call me when it's all done."

***

Cari walked into the kitchen and sat down with her mother and Mary Grace.

"Where's Brian?" Cari asked.

"He took our kids to school and then went to the church office. How was your walk?" Mary Grace inquired.

"Strange," Cari answered.

"How?" Beth asked. Something didn't feel right to her.

"I felt like I was followed. I didn't see anyone, but I kept getting this distinct impression that I was being followed. Like some kind of inner voice talking to me. I guess I'm just picking up on everyone's paranoia," she said.

Mary Grace slipped out her chair and went into the living room. She pulled open a slat from the blinds and peered outside. She could see a black car parked on the other side of the bushes in the front of her house. Her driveway was long and went uphill. If the car pulled in there might be enough time for Beth, Cari, and the kids to escape. She hoped it didn't pull in.

"I think Cari may be right. Cari, tell me something. What did you do on your little walks yesterday and today?" Mary Grace quizzed.

"Nothing," Cari lied.

"I hope you didn't make any phone calls, because if you did you just put your life and your kid's lives in danger," my friend said to her.

"God no!" Cari screamed. "I did call someone. I didn't believe any of you, so I called my friend Jeanna back home."

"The one who is the secretary at a Catholic church?" Beth asked.

"Yes," Cari said with tears forming in her eyes.

"Call her now and see if two priests stopped in to see her," Beth commanded.

Cari picked up the phone and dialed Jeanna's number. "Jeanna, this is Cari. I don't have time to talk. Just answer a question. Did two priests come in and ask about me?"

"Yeah, yesterday, but I thought—"

Cari smashed the phone down on the cradle.

"I screwed up, Mom. What now?"

Mary Grace grabbed her car keys from the hook by the door and yelled back to Beth and Cari. "Grab the kids and use the back door get away plan. A bus should be by in about five minutes. Take it to the house that Brian told you to find. I'll catch up to you there." She bolted out the door and jumped into her Jeep Cherokee Sport. Her wheels were spinning and throwing dirt as the two priests pulled into the driveway.

Cari grabbed the kids and raced out the back door, with Beth carrying whatever luggage she could. The four ran through the backyard and then out to the next street. The bus stop was only a few feet away.

Behind her Beth could hear the sound of crashing metal as Mary Grace rammed her Jeep into the front of the assassins' car. She could hear Mary Grace's screams and then a gun shot. Everything went silent as the bus pulled to a stop in front of them.

For there shall arise false Christs, and false prophets, and shall show great signs and wonders; so that, if it were possible, they shall deceive the very elect.
— Matthew 24:24

CHAPTER 26

I had stayed hidden most of the day so no one could see me approach the old gray stone church. The sun had just set as I peered through the window. I watched Father Brown get up from his old uncomfortable office chair to head to the rural mailbox outside his little parish church. He later told me he still couldn't figure out why they had to move the mailboxes to the street, or why his body hurt so much when he went there...or more precisely, when he went anywhere. Maybe it was those old football injuries from years ago at Notre Dame. If it wasn't for the priesthood Brown would've gone pro, but his calling seemed a little higher than the gridiron. He had been recruited and he'd thought about it, but Fred looked on it as a temptation.

For a man in his late seventies, besides the aches and pains, he was still in good shape...at times even robust. His hulking body appeared humorous behind the lectern on Sundays, but it worked to his advantage when it came to handling the neighborhood teens at the sports outreach.

Brown opened the door and moved down the stairs to the sidewalk. He was daring that night and crossed the street without looking both ways. He stepped from the curb and eased across the street. His shadow moved more quickly than he did, as the light source shifted from one street light to the next. There was no sound of cars to disturb a person's weary thoughts. Father Fred mumbled that there was never any traffic, and sometimes very little even on Sunday. He'd been sent to reestablish the parish in a changing community. Father Brown's warmth, vitality, and wisdom made for good relationships. Couple that with his intense spiritual sensitivity, and churches grew healthy under his pastoral care. St. Luke's needed to grow healthy again. The Italians and Irish, who once made up the congregation, had since moved to the north hill of the city, or out to the townships. The center of town had changed. The old stores were burning down and being replaced by empty parking lots. Not only had the people moved to the outlying areas, but so had their money.

Fred Brown was deep in thought as he snapped open the half crushed box and reached for his mail. He pulled four envelopes from the receptacle and thumbed through them. He mumbled how surprised he was that all four were in such good shape. Usually the postal system destroyed at least one quarter of his mail. "Just for principle," he mumbled. The third letter was from the Vatican. Brown inserted his finger inside the glued flap and had begun to rip the envelope open when I suddenly touched his shoulder. He spun around quickly like a cat...an old one, but still a cat.

"Father Brown?" I asked.

"What? Yes?" Brown knew my face but he couldn't believe I was there on his street. For a moment he studied me in the poor lighting with his weary eyes. "Oh my goodness, it's Matt MacDonald. It is you, isn't it? I haven't seen you in years. Not since the last time I visited your mom, just before she died." Brown grabbed me quickly and gave my tired body a bone-crushing bear hug. The old priest hadn't lost a bit of his strength. "What brings you here? And how in the world did you find me in New Castle, Pennsylvania?"

"Actually, you're the one that told me. When we met last, you said they were transferring you here. Anyway, it's good to see you, Father Brown." My mind felt relieved that Brown hadn't heard anything at that time about the situation I was in.

The old priest stepped back and gazed at my disheveled form from foot to head. He noticed the bag next to my feet, the pack on my back, and the exhausted look on my face. "You're in trouble, aren't you? And you look like you haven't slept for a couple days. What's happening, Matt?"

"Can we go inside and talk?"

"Sure." Fred picked up the bag and the two of us walked across the empty street. "Let's go into my study and talk for a bit. Can I get you something to eat or drink?"

I declined as we entered the building and walked to the room off the altar used as Brown's study. As we walked, I looked around. I wondered what he knew and didn't know. "Nice old building, Father Fred. How do you like it here?"

"This is sort of semi-retirement for me. The parish is small but it's a great old building. They don't build them like this anymore. I feel like I'm in some old, medieval castle. It has nooks, crannies, secret passages, and a small, very manageable parish for an old priest. But I'm sure this isn't an official visit to talk about my present pastoral situation. Unless of course, you have some kind of personal in with the new pope-in-waiting."

I grimaced as we entered Brown's study. Fred dropped my bag as I collapsed in a large, soft chair against the wall across from the door. Fred sat behind his big desk and looked again at me. It had been about five years since we'd seen each other. The last he'd heard, I was in Europe working as a biologist and doing especially well.

Brown slouched in the worn, blue leather chair across from me. "What's the problem, Matt? Is this a police thing? Are you running from them?"

"No, it's much bigger than that," I said as my mouth stretched in a wide yawn. My drooping eyes looked at Brown. I knew that I had to tell him, but the lack of sleep over the last few days seemed more oppressive to me than the two priests that were out to eliminate my existence. "I'll need lots of time to explain it to you. Right now, I haven't slept in a few days and I could use a bed. I'll be glad to tell you everything in the morning. I want you to know that I need some help and you are one of the few friends I have left. And right now, I trust very few people." I drawled out the words in exhausted phrases.

Fred Brown's heart was the only thing larger than his hulking body. He stood up and grabbed the bag again and said, "Then let me take you to your room, sir." I started to laugh.

Brown snickered out, "What's so funny?"

"I don't know. It might be that I'm so tired, but you reminded me of Lurch in that old Addams Family TV show." I felt myself growing more tired as I relaxed. It was good to be with Father Brown, the priest that had taught me about ethics, caring, and God. I felt like I had gotten so far from the God that Fred had so carefully and lovingly explained to me. To be back in Father Brown's presence reminded me of the basics of the faith that the old priest had taught. I felt safe — at least for now.

"Let me get you upstairs to a room." Brown was standing and smiling. I pulled my body out of the chair. I really didn't need a bed. The chair was soft enough after all the hours of hiding and running. I got up and moved toward the study door.

Fred grabbed me by the arm and said, "No, not that way. There is a back staircase from my study up to the bedrooms. Remember, I said this place is like an old castle. It was a way for priests to move from their private quarters upstairs to the offices downstairs in a mysterious way. This kept those little, old, superstitious ladies guessing about their priest's near divinity."

Brown walked over to the panel behind the soft chair, pressed a latch near the molding, and pushed back on the panel. We entered a small dimly lit hallway. Fred Brown had to slouch to walk through the low ceilinged passage. One bare, low-watt bulb lit the area to the stairs. Once we turned the corner, another bulb at the top of the stairs cast its yellowing glow along the shadowed steps. Father Brown was right about the building seeming medieval. As he reached the top of the stairs, Brown hit another latch that opened the panel into the hallway. Before we stepped through, Fred stopped, turned to me, and said, "Wait a second. I've got to show you this. When the old church was built, the architect put in this closet over here to store valuable relics and items. When I moved in I found it by accident."

"And inside was the body of one of the apostles?" I quipped.

"No, nothing that exciting. I found some old altar ware. They were solid gold. I hate to say it, but I sold them, and that's how we built the basketball courts out there for the neighborhood kids to play on." Fred smiled about that. That act went hand-in-hand with Father Brown's value system. He was a man of God and a man of the people. Then we walked into the hallway to the bedrooms. I fell on the bed the moment we walked in without taking off my clothes. In seconds I was asleep. Brown grabbed the blanket laying on the dresser and covered me. In those last moments before I hit a deep, long-needed sleep, I heard Brown wonder out loud, "What in the world are you into, Matt?" Tomorrow, I would tell him. It could wait.

The old priest headed back down the stairway and into his study, and Brown noticed his unopened letters on the desk and the overnight express from the Vatican. Later he told me he had hoped it wasn't some ridiculous change that would upset his small congregation any further. His age made change hard, but his desire to be obedient to the authorities above him made it difficult not to uphold what was required of him, especially in a time of such turmoil in the Vatican. He pulled the letter from the envelope and scanned down the page.

Dear Father Brown,

Somewhere in your past ministry, you have made contact with one Matthew MacDonald. Mr. MacDonald has lived for several years in Zurich, Switzerland and worked for the Amrich

THE SIGN OF THE END

Corporation. He was also subcontracted by the Vatican to assist in the Messiah project. We have, in recent days, lost contact with Mr. MacDonald, and fear that he is being persuaded by a radical underground militia to compromise his Catholic beliefs in order to take part in a wicked plot against our Holy Catholic Church. He may be insane.

If, for some reason, Matthew MacDonald should contact you for aid in his flight or his plot, please inform the bishop of your archdiocese immediately. It is our desire to help Matthew find the psychiatric and spiritual aid he needs before he is arrested by international police forces. Please help Matthew by helping us. Thank you.

In Your Service,
Archbishop John Russo
Vatican City

Brown was shocked, and read the letter again. "So this explains Matt's situation. I can't believe it though. What should I do? I need to call. I need to help Matt." Brown raised the phone to his ear and punched in the number of the bishop.

"Hello, this is Father Fred Brown at St. Luke's in New Castle. May I speak with the bishop please?"

The voice on the other end rudely answered, "And what makes you think he's taking calls this late at night? Can't this wait till tomorrow morning?"

Fred attempted to keep a poised and pleasant voice over his angry attitude. "I was instructed by the Vatican to call the bishop if I came into contact with a Matthew MacDonald. He has shown up at my parish and I am following the directives of the Vatican. I've done what I'm supposed to do. May I speak with him now?"

The voice on the other end retorted, "I'll give him the message. Good-bye." The line went dead.

Frustrated and confused, Brown stood up, turned off the light to his study, and moved through the hidden passage to his bedroom. He wondered what he should do next. He needed to hear my story, but that wouldn't be until the morning. Had he done the right thing in calling? After knowing me and all my family for so many years, it just didn't seem logical that one of the brightest young men he had ever known could have fallen into something so evil in his middle age. He sat over his journal at his bedroom desk, struggling for the words to express his inner turmoil with those hard questions.

...be on your guard... — I Peter 3:17

CHAPTER 27

The sun had already been up for three hours before I awoke. Father Brown had finished the morning mass and cooked breakfast for the two of us. He was carrying a tray of food into the study when I pushed open the passage door. Brown looked at me strangely. I suppose he still couldn't believe what he had read. He spoke, "Good morning, Matthew. How does eggs, hash browns, toast, and bacon sound? And of course, lots of coffee, because I have a feeling that you have quite a story to tell me. So why don't you begin at the beginning and fill me in?"

We sat down at his small old wooden table. I told him about cloning an egg from the Shroud of Turin DNA samples and the years that followed. Much of this could be gathered from city newspapers, Catholic newsletters, and continuous coverage in the major news magazines. Nothing new except when I spoke of my meetings with Jesus. "Father Fred, there was something that I could never figure out. I knew how to create an exact replica of Jesus physically, but what about the soul? If it's given by God, if it's our connection to Him, then how in the world could this Jesus have one? I could do the physical, but not the spiritual."

Brown had no answer. He told me there was something he could not pinpoint that had always gnawed at his trust in this new Jesus. When I asked the question, he realized what caused that mistrust — he had never felt any spiritual link to this Messiah.

I continued. "A few weeks ago, Thompson and Bishop Russo brought the clone to me again. Something was wrong. They wanted me to fix him. They acted like I was running some kind of auto mechanic shop and they were bringing him in under warranty."

Brown laughed.

"I started to examine him, and found that his body was deteriorating. I couldn't figure out what was happening to him. Why would the body deteriorate, and why was I glad of it?"

Brown looked at me like I was making a lot of sense in my confusion. I knew there was a lack in my understanding of God and the way we were created. Father Brown asked me, "Matt, if God has ordained our lives to live for a certain period of time, and if this is truly Jesus's DNA make-up, wouldn't it have been designed to live only this long?"

I was sure my eyes sparkled with revelation. I felt like it was the first reflection of the old Matthew in days. "Father Brown, you may be absolutely right. You have confirmed what was shown to me before. If this is Jesus's body, then more than likely he has only a few months, at the most, left. He is destined to die. Then there is nothing I can do about it. Now, there's one more big question to answer. What about the two priests that are chasing me around the country?"

"The what?"

"Well, after I told Thompson and Russo that I couldn't do anything, I also voiced my feeling that I couldn't sense any spiritual presence from him. They asked me if I could meet them the next day for one final exam. I then got a call from the Director of the CIA, and he led me to believe I was in danger. Maybe it was because I've always suspected that it was Jesus that poisoned the pope that I was inclined to believe the CIA. Anyway, I grabbed my family and escaped to the States. They're in hiding until I find us a safe house."

Brown quizzed further. "How do you know they're after you?"

"After we left Zurich, our house was broken into. The neighbor who told me about it said two priests came by, one dark haired, one light colored. I kept thinking that Starsky and Hutch from the old TV show were after me. Then here in the U.S. I was meeting with one of my former grad school professors in a restaurant in Philadelphia. Two priests entered and sat at a table near us. When they walked in they looked at me several times and spoke quietly to each other. I was looking for two guys that looked like Starsky and Hutch, and wouldn't you know it, they didn't disappoint me. I mentioned it to the professor. He had a flaming appetizer ordered for their table. When it came, the old guy tripped the waiter. The scalding liquids went all over the so-called priests. While they were screaming, I slipped out the back through the kitchen. I've been running ever since. That's why I showed up last night so exhausted." As I finished, I poured myself another cup of coffee.

I could tell Brown was very confused. Looking back now, I'm sure he was thinking that there was a great discrepancy between what he read in the letter the night before and what he'd heard the next morning. He decided to ask some questions. "Matt, are you sure they just don't want you to return and help them find a cure? Maybe you'd do best by going back and settling this issue."

"Archbishop Russo made it very clear that he understood there was nothing I could do. He also said that I was to keep silent about what I knew or they would make sure I stayed silent. I think he meant permanently. At first it only infuriated me. Then Thompson started asking about my family in a very intimidating way. They already knew where my daughter lived and how many grandchildren I had. I figured then that they were serious. That's why my family's in hiding and I'm running across the country."

"Matthew," Brown started to confess. "Yesterday I received a letter from the Vatican. I didn't open it until after you went to bed. The letter's view of the story is quite different. To them you are mentally unbalanced and part of a plot to destroy this Messiah you created. It asked me to call the bishop in Pittsburgh." He paused and my heart thumped with terror. Brown continued, "So I did."

As we spoke a news story flashed on the television Father Brown had in the kitchen. The story was out of Philadelphia. The talking head had a perplexed look on his face as he reported. According to the story, two men disguised as priests had attempted a hold up on a small Philly cafe. In the confusion an elderly college professor was shot and killed. When they mentioned Dr. Grant's name, both the father and I gasped simultaneously.

"Father Brown, did you hear that? That means your phone call will bring the killers to this door. They could be here any minute. Why did you do that? This could mean my life," I screamed as I jumped up.

Father Brown stood up and walked to me. He grabbed me by the shoulders and spoke loud and fast into my face. "Matthew, I'm sorry. But how do I know that your story is true? I mean, two priests that look like Starsky and Hutch chasing you across the nation just to kill you seems a little far out there. Maybe you do need some help."

Brown heard the front door of the church open and spun away from me. He must've forgotten to lock it after the morning mass. I heard it too. Fear stiffened my body. The priest moved to the little window that looked out into the sanctuary, with me right behind him. We saw two figures walking up the darkened side aisle. As they walked through the rays of stained glass sunlight we got a look at them. Two priests…one was dark haired, one light colored. It was the two killers.

As they approached the altar and the door to his study, the priests reached into their coats and pulled out hand guns. Brown had less than ten seconds to think of something and to react while I moved toward the secret passageway.

The old priest placed his bulking arms under the desk, a desk obviously too small for a former Notre Dame lineman. I watched silently as the door opened. The fake priests entered with guns drawn, ready to silence me. At that moment, Father Brown lifted his desk off the ground and hurled it at the two while he yelled at me to run. The old wooden desk struck the two and knocked them to the floor. One instinctively aimed his gun at Brown and fired two shots. One struck him in the side, and as the gun recoiled, the other pierced his shoulder.

In the midst of the mayhem, I undid the latch to the door into the hidden passage, passed into the hallway, and snapped the door back into place. Inside, I was torn between going back to aid Father Brown or staying hidden. I heard the sound of the two priests beating on the wall, and that made my decision for me. I had already prepared for an escape route. It was becoming more of a second nature to me. I reached up and broke the bulb in the hallway, and then raced for the stairway. At the top I undid the latch to the storeroom designed to hide the expensive relics and liturgical utensils. As I smashed the light bulb near it, I heard the two open the door below. I slipped inside and hoped that in the dark no one would discover me.

Soteri yelled at Chuckie the Hat, "Why did you shoot the priest? That noise is going to bring the cops."

They stopped and the Hat spoke. "I can't see a thing. It was tough enough to find that latch in a lighted room. He's probably upstairs and out a window by now."

Soteri retorted, "We've got less than five minutes to find him before this place is crawling with uniforms. Go back through the old man's study and find the other staircase to the rectory. I'll continue searching here. If he left then he couldn't have gotten far. We should be able to track him down by evening."

I heard him climb the staircase and paw at the door to the hallway. Those few moments seemed like an eternity, then I heard the Hat open the rectory hallway passage door.

"Any sign of him?" asked Soteri.

"Nothing. He got out of here already or he disappeared into thin air," said the Hat. "Let's split. The cops will be here in a few minutes."

I sucked in a deep breath and let it out as I heard them depart. In the small hidden room I noticed a window. I pressed easily to open it so I could watch and hear the street below.

Before long the police arrived. The first officer that arrived on the scene was Big Tony Marone. I learned their names later. He coasted into the area with his headlights off, and parked one hundred feet east of the building. I could hear Marone radio to his backup officer to come in from the west and take a position to cover that side. Forty-five seconds later, Jimmy Smith took up his position. I saw Marone frown and spit over the dispatcher's choice of backup for him. When he saw Smith, Marone uttered the word "boot," because Smith had only been on the streets two weeks. Marone told Smith where he wanted him and what he wanted him to do. "Stay out of the way and keep your mouth shut." Big Tony's concern was that Smith would get his stupid rookie head shot off, and Tony didn't want to lose another cop to a dumb mistake.

Once Smith was in position, Marone radioed his dispatcher and asked her to call the Church to make phone contact with someone inside. Marone didn't rush into things, and had a reputation for going cautiously by the book. Big Tony wanted to know who was inside and if anyone was hurt. Most of these calls turned out to be firecrackers or cars backfiring, but then Big Tony hadn't gotten to be as old or as big as he was by assuming anything.

It seemed like an hour to Marone outside and me inside, but only a few minutes passed before dispatch radioed back that there was a busy signal. Dispatch had asked the operator to do an emergency break-through.

The operator reported that the phone must be off the hook.

"Criminy," said Tony. "This is not good." His skin started to crawl. He didn't want to make entry without more backup, but he was concerned for any injuries inside that could use immediate attention. Marone radioed his dispatch again and asked for two more officers and for a paramedic unit to stand by in case they were needed. He knew fast medical treatment was important, but rushing in without more help could make them dead. "And dead ain't no help to anyone," he mumbled.

Within minutes of Marone's request for help, the back-up, John Toronski and Ray Weber, came. Weber said to Toronski, "If Big Tony is asking for more officers then something big is going on." Everyone knew Tony had an uncanny way of smelling trouble. Both Toronski and Weber were veterans and with them, Tony knew it would be S.O.P.

Big Tony looked at Toronski. "Take your position on the southeast corner. That way you can watch both the front and the east side of the building." Turning to Smith, he barked, "Stay where you are on the northwest corner so you can observe the west side and rear of the building." Marone breathed a cop's prayer that Smith would do what he was told and keep his eyes wide open. Boots made mistakes.

Big Tony was ready to make entry to the building. He and Weber approached the front doors cautiously. Weber said he was surprised that his hands still went clammy after all these years. Tony had his pistol drawn and at the ready while Ray had the twelve gauge in his cold, sweaty hands. Marone seemed at ease having Ray back him up with the twelve gauge Remington pump.

I moved over to a peep hole cut in the wall overlooking the sanctuary. I had a feeling that this room was once used for more than storage. When they entered the dark church, Tony went low and to the left. Ray went high and to the right and swept the interior, looking for any potential threats. They went down separate aisles and kept each other in sight while Tony used his flashlight to shine a quick flash on shadowed areas. They didn't want the light to pinpoint their location. Tony's training officer used to say, "Bad guys like it when you advertise your location." Searches made Tony tense, but like any cop he loved the adrenaline rush.

Once they cleared the pews, the two came to the door of Father Brown's study. At this point I could no longer see, but their conversation told me all I needed to know. The door was slightly open and strangely lit. The light radiated up from the floor, casting eerie shadows in the room. According to police procedure, Tony looked at Ray and nodded to the door. Ray knew this meant they were going to make entry, with Tony low on the left and Ray high on the right.

I could hear the sound of gun metal on wood as Ray reached out for the door, touching it with the barrel of the shotgun and slowly pushing it. As the door creaked open, the source of the odd lighting came into view. The desk was turned over and the lamp had fallen to the floor, with its shade cocked at an angle. Their eyes raced around the room quickly, looking for perps. Nobody was seen, but they still entered cautiously and spread out in opposite directions from the doorway. As Ray moved to the right, Marone noticed him stop and stare at the floor behind the desk. Weber looked up at Tony, and his large saddened eyes said "It isn't good," even before he stated it.

Tony took a few steps toward the desk, and at his feet was the lifeless body of Father Brown, laying on his side. He had attempted to scratch out words on the carpet in his own blood. It looked like an "M," a "T" and the numbers two, four, two, and four again. Big Tony moved forward and checked the priest's carotid artery for a pulse, but there was none. The two couldn't help Brown and they had to finish their search. They whispered that the killer may still be in the building, and neither one wanted to be the next victim, so they continued the search. I crouched low and quiet in my hiding place, praying they would not discover me.

When Tony was satisfied that there wasn't a threat to himself or the other officers, he picked up his radio and said "code four." It was secure. Marone then called the dispatcher. "Got a probable homicide. Notify the homicide detective and the coroner." With that done, Tony sent Jimmy Smith and John Toronski to the rectory to search for clues. Before they went, Tony called to them, "Hey guys, be careful, or what you see here could be you." Toronski would keep Smith out of trouble and look out for the kid. Tony had Weber wait outside for homicide and the coroner while he took notes in the dead priest's study concerning what he had seen. When more officers arrived. Marone sent them to interview the person who had reported the shots and to check the neighborhood for other possible witnesses.

Through my peephole and the open front door, I could see Charley Elliot's car ease up to the front of the church. Elliot swung from his car and walked up to Weber, who was scribbling his notes. "Hi, Charley," said Weber as he looked up from his notepad and wrote down the time Elliot had arrived. "Somebody's whacked the old priest, Father Brown. The study was tossed. My guess is that it's a robbery that got botched. Big Tony's inside with the body. Hey, how could someone do that to a priest?"

Elliot grumbled and went into the church. He knew exactly where the study was since he had been an altar boy there years ago, lots of years ago.

Walking into the study, he saw Marone sitting in the chair in the far corner writing in his pad. Marone barely looked up at Elliot. "Charley, we got a bucket for ya this time."

Elliot grunted back, "What yinz got, 'T'?"

Big Tony detailed the story, which is where I got a lot of what I've been able to write. "When we got inside, we found Father Brown just as you see him. He had bled out before we got to him. He started writing something over here. I can't quite make it out, just letters and numbers is all I can see."

Charley recognized the bloody scribbles as a Bible reference to Matthew 24:24, and was jotting a note to look it up when Jimmy Smith walked in.

"A Bible verse? Hey, I know that one. 'For there shall arise false Christs, and false prophets, and shall show great signs and wonders; insomuch that, if it were possible, they shall deceive the very elect.'"

Tony and Elliot stared at Smith as if he were from an alien planet. Elliot quizzed, "Are you sure, kid?" The reference was more important than anyone else would know. It gave Elliot a good idea of what had happened.

"Twelve years in AWANA. We had to learn verses all the time. Matthew 24:24 was one of them. Actually, I'm kind of amazed that I remembered it," Smith said with a look of pride before Big Tony waved him out of the room.

Tony continued to speak. "I'm sorry, I know the two of you used to work together with the neighborhood kids." Elliot grunted again and walked around the room. Tony added his assessment. "Looks to me like someone tried to maybe burg the place and the priest caught him."

"Could be," Elliot answered. Charley wasn't known to be that talkative at a crime scene. He was busy looking at everything trying to put things together and see what the facts said, not what people supposed. "This ain't no bungled burg or robbery," he said as he noticed the dishes and food from two meals. "Someone was here with Father Brown. Where's the other person?" Elliot asked Marone. I started to sweat in my little room.

"What are you talking about, Charley?"

"Look here. We've got plates and food for two people, and its fresh. I can still smell the bacon in the air."

Marone's embarrassed response was evident. "I didn't even notice. I guess that's why they pay you the big bucks, huh? The place is clear though. We searched it and found nothing."

"Search it again and look for anything that might tell us who was here with the victim," Elliot barked. The body was no longer Father Brown to Charley. He was just "the victim." That was Elliot's way of avoiding emotional involvement. He needed to remain open minded and objective, and the only way he could do that was to see each person as the "victim." Brown was just the "victim," a case that needed to be solved. Charley asked, "Did the lady who called in see anything?"

Another cop stepped into the room. He overheard the question and interrupted. "Detective, I just came back from the neighbor's house. She only saw a car with two men in it speeding away."

212

Elliot was irritated that he would have to ask for more information and barked out, "So what did the guys look like? What did the car look like? Do we have an APB out on this yet? Come on, guys, don't wait around for me to ask all the questions. Give me the info."

The officer flipped open his pad and started to rattle off, "She's pretty old and her eyes ain't good. But she did say it was a dark, late-model car about midsized with two men, white guys, both dressed in black or some kinda dark color."

"Is there an APB out on this?"

"My partner is calling it in now."

"Good work. Now has anyone bothered to check the passageway up to the rectory?" Charley asked. My fear turned to nausea when I heard this.

From all the blank stares, Elliot knew they weren't even aware of the old secret passage. Charley moved to the wall. "I used to be an altar boy here in St. Luke's, years and years ago. Every once in a while, the priest back then would send me upstairs to get stuff he forgot. There's this passageway from the study up to the rectory. Look at this, officers; let me give you a lesson in detective work. See the scratches along here? It looks like someone was furiously looking for the latch that opens the door." He popped it open. "Give me a flashlight."

One of the officers brought over his police issue. Elliot grabbed it and flashed the light inside. "Gentlemen, can you see the broken bulb glass on the floor? Whoever it was escaped through here and probably out an upstairs window. Which explains why there's two meals down in the study. Check the upstairs rooms for some kinda sign of a visitor."

I listened intently. I figured the detective didn't know about the secret compartment or he would've been up the stairs in a minute to find his witness or murderer. I sat and listened.

One of the officers returned with my bag and spoke to Elliot. "Found this upstairs in one of the rooms. There are some papers inside that belong to a Matthew MacDonald."

"Matthew MacDonald. I hearda him. Wonder why he was here," questioned Elliot. Most likely, his mind started flashing through the evidence like a video in fast forward. He turned to the other cops and closed the passage. "I was wrong. The cobwebs haven't been disturbed. Nobody's been in there for a while." Upstairs, I sighed.

"How do you know him, Charley?" asked Marone.

"He's the guy that did the cloning of Jesus," he answered.

"How do you know that?"

"I read. Something you Neanderthals should try." Charley Elliot was a decorated war veteran. Over the years, he'd grown disillusioned with life, religion, and politics. In the past few months, he'd gotten involved with the Quaker State Movement, a small group of dissenting patriots that didn't see the nation's alignment with the cloned Messiah as a good thing.

"From what I heard, this MacDonald guy told some church groups out east that this Jesus clone ain't kosher. But most likely, you guys don't know or care about that stuff." Charley stopped talking then picked up another conversation. "So are we done here?" Elliot asked as they carried out Brown's body.

"All through, Detective."

"Okay, I'm gonna stay around for a few more minutes and see if we missed anything. Leave MacDonald's bag for me to go through," Elliot requested.

In a few minutes the police cars pulled away. I still heard one set of footsteps walking around. Then the steps moved down the passageway and up the stairs toward the hiding place. I heard his fingers on the latch to my hiding place. It opened and the dimly lit face of Detective Charley Elliot was staring me in the eyes. I looked down and saw the detective's gun pointed at me. My heart stopped for a moment, and I could feel tears of fear come to my eyes. I was caught. It was over.

Hide me from the secret counsel of the wicked; from the insurrection of the workers of iniquity: —Psalm 64:2

CHAPTER 28

"Dr. MacDonald, I presume," Elliot said with a smile.

I raised my hands and sighed. It was over. I expected to be shot at any moment.

"Yeah, what are you going to do with me?" I asked.

"Get ya outta town, Doc. There's some people out there that would love ta knock ya off. And this is one cop that ain't gonna let that three dollar bill Jesus do it to ya. Now, put your hands down and tell me what's going on."

We went back to Father Fred's office and I sat there telling the cop what had happened. I gave him the whole story. I figured someone had to know the trail of terror and murder that was being left behind the fake priests. Then I asked him, "Detective, why aren't you turning me in? And how do you know about the Messiah's true nature?"

"There's a lot of us out there that don't trust our government or this one world government that Jesus and that almost Pope Russo are tryin' to pull together. We've tried to stop it before, but you were the one that ruined our best chance."

"Disney World?" I said as both a question and a statement.

"You got it, Doc. And now that you have seen the light, it's my duty to make sure that you live long enough to get the truth about this one world government into the hands of the public. First we got to get you outta here. I figure those two killers in collars are sittin' out there waitin' for ya to leave. When ya do, they'll be there."

"So what do we do?" I asked.

"I'll take you to my old partner's house. He lives out in the township. Great lookin' country around here. If anyone follows us, I'll shake 'em. Once we know it's safe, then we'll get ya to the airport," Elliot said.

"Why the airport?"

"Our movement has a network of safe houses around the country. I'll set it up for ya to have a place you can hide. It will be jist about untraceable."

"Even from the CIA?" I asked.

"Especially those idiots," Charlie said.

"Listen, Elliot, you're the only chance I've got right now. But what about my family?"

"Are they safe right now?" he asked.

"Yeah, I guess so."

"Tell me where they are and we'll get them to you, 'cos they won't be safe for long," he warned.

"They're with a pastor from a dissenting church," I said.

"The one in Riverdale, Maryland?" he asked. "They ain't safe no more. Two guys attacked the place yesterday and shot the pastor's wife. No one else was found. The only description of the perps was that it was two guys dressed in black. I heard somebody report that they were supposed to look like Starsky and Hutch."

I didn't say a word. I simply began to cry with heavy sobs. Mary Grace was dead because I had dragged her into my problems. Her death made up my mind. I was going to use Elliot's contacts to find a safe house and have my family brought to me. After that, all communications about the Messiah, Russo, and Thompson would dry up. No more info. No more people would die.

As the evening's darkness thickened we headed for Elliot's unmarked police car. He pulled out and we started to head west out of town. In a few minutes he spoke.

"It looks like we got company. Two guys in a car behind us. They are staying a good distance away. These two are pros. This just ain't two priests that decided to do a Thelma and Louise impersonation. We got two trained killers behind us. It looks like the evening is going to get more exciting. Hang on. I'm going to lose them."

Elliot whipped his car onto a dark dirt road and then over a small bridge. We fishtailed into a left turn and climbed a hill lined with trees on both sides. He kept glancing up into the mirror as we raced over the road.

"Those boys are good. I guess I'll have to use my more advanced evasion tactics," he said, with his grin showing in the green glow of the dashboard light.

Elliot and I bounced out of our seats each time he crested another small hill in the unmarked police car. It had the engine power to stay in the lead, but it struck me that it was infinitely easier to follow a car on a dark, bumpy, dirt road than it was to see the upcoming twists and turns. Something told me though that Charlie Elliot had run this road before.

We had just made a sharp bend when Charlie pushed off the headlights. I was afraid to say a word as the detective maneuvered the car into a bare spot along the side of the dirt road. I watched as he turned around and got back on the road heading right for our pursuers. Then he stopped the car and waited. It was difficult to see his face, but I could hear him well in the country quiet.

"I'm going to do something that they'll never suspect. The other driver is going to slow down to try and find this turn off. He'll find it okay, and then he'll coast into the road heading right at us. The two will have been looking at the side of the road away from the light. A bright light at this point will blind them. He'll pull in and I'll snap on the high beams and my searchlight. It will give us about ten seconds to blow right by him, and that will give me enough time to get a few shots off. Are you ready?"

"I guess so, but what if they get a few shots off as well?" I asked.

"Little chance of that, but just in case duck down in your seat." He stopped talking and then whispered, "There they are."

Elliot flashed on his lights, and I saw the other car swerve onto the side of the road. It looked like they had run into a ditch. In another three seconds we were right on top of their car. Charlie's window was down and his hand held his service revolver. I saw the flashes of light escape from the barrel as he shot three times into the other car.

We came to the end of the road and Charlie whipped the car to the left and turned out his lights again. This time he hurtled down the dark road with no lights. The black night and the clouds of dust made us impossible to see. Then without warning he turned the car sharply into a driveway that seemed to be obscured from the road by bushes. I wondered how he knew where it was.

"Welcome to the Quaker Movement's Summer Camp, Doc. It will be a miracle if they find this road, and a bigger one if they can get through the security gate." He pushed an electronic button that sat in the middle of a piece of black plastic hanging from his key chain. The gate opened and we passed through. We went another mile down the road and I saw a small cabin nestled in the middle of several pine trees.

"What's here?" I asked. I still didn't trust Elliot. In fact, I was starting not to trust anyone.

"Our people do some training on these secluded acres. My old partner from the force stays here and guards the camp from snoops and feds. You'll like old Ed. He's about 6'7" and built like a brick wall. Between the two of us we'll figure out a way to get you out of this place and then to somewhere safe."

We stopped on the far side of the cabin and climbed out. In the dark I could see a figure standing in the doorway with an automatic rifle in his hands.

"Charlie, wassup? What yinz doin' 'ere?" Ed called to us.

"We got a very important guest, Big Ed. Meet Matthew MacDonald, the guy that did the cloning on Jesus," Elliot said as we crossed the grass to the front porch of the cabin.

"Nice to meet you, Mr. MacDonald. I was just watchin' yer clone on the boob tube," Ed said.

"Nice to meet you as well, but why is he on TV?" I asked.

"Hey, I guess it's already Good Friday over in Israel and he's preachin' to the whole world. It just started. Sit and watch it while I get ya both sumptin to eat," Big Ed told us as he motioned me to a seat near the television.

"Nothin' for me, Eddy. I gotta use the communications gear and get this boy a safe house far away from here." Elliot continued through the room and through a door, and I could hear him go down a set of stairs. I sucked in a deep breath and relaxed as my clone's voice spoke. I could see the strain in his eyes when the cameras came in for a close-up. More importantly, his speaking lacked its normal power. It almost seemed disjointed and unlinked, something I had never heard before from the Messiah.

*And I saw one of his heads as it were wounded to death;
and his deadly wound was healed: and all the world
wondered after the beast. — Revelation 13:3*

CHAPTER 29

Prophet Thompson, Archbishop Russo, and several
Israeli government and religious leaders sat on the
platform looking at Jesus as he continued to speak. Russo
stretched his arms out behind him, and at that precise
moment there was a shot from the crowd of worshipers
and listeners.

Jesus stopped in mid-word. His eyes went from
stunned to a blank, dead stare, then his body fell over
backwards, where a pool of blood immediately formed
underneath his head. The shot had gone straight through
his brain from its entry point between the eyes.

Everyone scrambled to their feet. The crowd panicked
and stampeded. People were thrown to the ground and
trampled while others pushed and shoved their way to
some kind of perceived safety.

The cameras were trained all over the scene. Russo
was at the side of Jesus first. Thompson stood over them
in a protective stance. Both were physically shaken, and

Thompson's eyes were filling with tears. And each tear was caught on film as he looked right into the lens.

In the crowd of people, David Abraham stood with his rifle still in his hands, waiting for Joshua Longtree to step his way and fire the blank at his heart. In a moment, Longtree emerged from the crowd and walked towards David.

"Good shot. Now I'll fulfill our part of the bargain." Longtree raised his gun and pointed it right at Abraham's forehead. Suddenly he understood that the CIA agent's gun would not have a blank in it. It would have live ammunition.

Abraham attempted to raise his rifle to protect himself, but Longtree smiled and said, "You'll get your rewards in the next life. It's time to go meet those seventy-two virgins." Joshua fired. Abraham's eyes went from shocked to the same cold, dead stare that he'd given the Messiah.

***

I sat on the chair in the headquarters of the Quaker State Movement watching the clone I had created be gunned down. My mouth was wide open as Big Ed walked next to me and put his hand on my shoulder.

"I guess we don't have to worry about him anymore," Ed said.

I couldn't answer. Charlie Elliot came up from the bunker below the cabin.

"Got ya a safe house in California," the detective said.

"He may not need it," Ed said.

"Why? What's goin' on?" Just then he looked over at the TV and saw the news bulletin that the Messiah had been assassinated. "Holy crap! This is going to be some kinda mess. What's goin' on there, Matthew?"

"I, ah, ah, really don't know. Jesus was dying anyway and may have lasted only a few months. My thoughts are that Archbishop Russo had him shot," I answered.

"Why do somethin' like that?" Ed asked.

"A martyred Jesus will have more power than one who simply died from heart failure. I've got to hand it to Russo. He even turned this bad situation into gold." I sat back and rubbed my eyes with my hands. "Who knows what he'll do next?"

"I know what we gotta do next. We need to get you to the Pittsburgh airport," Charlie said.

"What if your company is waiting?" Ed asked.

"I already got that figured out. I'm going to put some kind of dummy in the car next to me and leave first. They'll follow me. Then a few minutes later you leave with the doc and get him to the airport. That's fairly simple, but like everything simple, it will work," Charlie told us.

Big Ed and I stuffed some of his old clothes with other old clothes and made a dummy. As Ed placed it in the car I went to thank Detective Elliot.

"I really appreciate what you've done for me. How will my family find me?"

"We already worked that out. Your wife, daughter, and grandkids are bein' hid by one of the dissenting churches in the D.C. area. They'll get them to the airport and one of our men will meet them in Orange County. He'll bring them to ya. But first we gotta get ya there. Now, let's go kick some assassin butt!"

Charlie climbed into the car and sped out the gate. It was only moments later that we heard gunshots. Starsky and Hutch must've been waiting outside the gate.

"Charlie's plan is workin'. Now, let's get ya outta here and down to Pittsburgh airport," Ed said. We climbed into his Ford Bronco and shot through the gate, heading the other way.

We weren't sure what was going on in the other direction, but I did hear later that Elliot led them on a high speed chase through the back roads again. This time, though, one of the two fake priests was able to get a good shot at Charlie. The bullet hit him, and Elliot lost control of the car and rammed a tree. It was obvious that he still wasn't dead because one of the two killers pumped one more bullet into his head. They also figured out how to open the gate at the camp. But by the time they discovered I wasn't there we were too far gone to catch, although Ed and I knew that their first guess would be the airport. Our only hope was that my plane would leave on time, and that would be too soon for them to catch me.

***

The entire world glued themselves to their TV sets. It was like a black shroud had fallen from heaven and obliterated the globe. Newscasters could not report without tears. And the only thing on the news was the assassination of the Prince of Peace.

Over and over the image of Jesus's eyes going from shocked to dead was played. Over and over the image of CIA agent Joshua Longtree subduing then having to shoot the assassin in self-defense would dance across the screen. Dead. Dead. Dead. It was truly the most important story of the century. Greater even than his birth.

It was only then that one could understand the full impact that the clone had on the peoples of Earth. He had become their link with God. With his death, the world saw

God die. In God's death they saw hope fade into the abyss.

The airport televisions carried the events. I could watch the teary eyed reports as I raced from waiting area to waiting area. One bit of information made me stop. Israel was apologizing to the world for this horrific event. They had decided to place a statue of the deceased Messiah not inside the city of Jerusalem as originally planned, but they had gotten permission to place it inside what is considered the original temple. At first it sounded like a wonderful gesture from a country's contrite heart. And that it truly was. But there was something else about that event. Something that nagged at my mind.

I moved on to my departure gate and waited. It looked like the plane would leave on time. There was a small store that had several books and magazines. I decided to grab something for my journey.

As I glanced over the books, my eyes were drawn to the religious section. In there I felt I'd find the answer to what nagged at my thoughts and memory. There was something very significant about the placement of the statue inside the original temple walls, but I didn't know what.

Then I spied the answer. There were two books side by side. The first was the Bible. I guessed it was time for me to closely examine it to see if the scriptures could shed some light on what was happening. The book next to it was thin. Its title was simple...*What the Bible Says About the End of the Age*. I snapped it up. Could there be any relation to what I was living through and what the Bible was predicting for the end of the earth? I had the whole flight to California to figure it out.

I bought the books and walked to my departure gate waiting area. They were already announcing our boarding. I got in line and waited. As the airline ticket clerk slipped my one way ticket from the folder and slid it into the outer pocket of the folder, something flashed by the corner of my eye. It was a light haired man in a black suit with a white parochial collar.

I quickly moved into the tunnel and headed to my seat. I had made it by only seconds. If he had seen me he could have made enough noise to delay the flight and had me detained. Since Big Ed had given me a false ID and the ticket was paid for in cash, there was little chance that they'd know what flight I had taken. A disturbance would delay the flight, and a passenger with a cash ticket and no luggage would be flagged right away.

I got to my seat next to the window and plopped down, then pulled the small book from the shopping bag and opened it up. The first chapter was entitled, "Are We In the End Times Now?" I could only shake my head and say, "yes."

And he deceives those who dwell on the earth by those signs which he was granted to do in the sight of the beast, telling those who dwell on the earth to make an image to the beast who was wounded by the sword and lived. He was granted power to give breath to the image of the beast, that the image of the beast should both speak and cause as many as would not worship the image of the beast to be killed. — Revelation 13:14-15

CHAPTER 30

The news was filled with further world events. Stocks were declining, people were committing suicide, all while Israel was negotiating with Archbishop Russo to have Jesus buried in the rock tomb thought to be the original tomb of Christ.

"We are greatly repentant, Archbishop. The original tomb site is being prepared as we speak. We will do whatever we can in this very heavy moment in world history. It is our desire that the world see us not as the cause of his death, but as his greatest grievers. We want the world to think of us as Joseph of Arimathea instead of as Judas Iscariot. Please, accept our gift of the tomb," the Israeli Prime Minister pleaded.

"I want you to know that Prophet Thompson and I do not hold you responsible for the actions of one madman. Your kindness and generosity are all we can ask. Although, we would like to know when you will be placing the memorial statue inside the original temple walls?" Russo said with a gleam in his eyes.

"We thought that your Easter Sunday holiday would be appropriate," the Israeli leader reported.

"That is fine," Russo said as he glanced at Thompson, giving him a sly, knowing smile. "I do have one request concerning the statue."

"Yes, Archbishop, just say it and it will be done," the Jewish government official said.

"I would like to have the statue brought to the hangar where my Lord Jesus's airplane is kept. I want to spend some time alone in worship, and it is very comforting to me."

"It is done."

Once the Israeli delegation left their hotel room, Thompson and Russo sat and spoke while Laura took notes of what had to be done.

"Once the statue arrives, have them switch it with the animatronic double, Laura," Thompson grunted. "This way we can deceive the hordes of pilgrims that flock to worship the statue of the Messiah. Isn't modern technology wonderful?"

"I still think we're taking a great risk in bringing in this many people who can leak the truth behind our upcoming miracle," the archbishop cautioned.

"Don't worry. Didn't you read in the newspaper about the horrible accident on Easter morning that took the life of several Italian and American pilgrims?" He smiled when he said it. It made Laura sick to think that more people would die. People that she could save if only she had enough courage to tell the world the truth. But she didn't. The closest she would ever come was giving me all the information she'd gathered, along with what Maria had given her out of the Vatican.

Once the slain body of Jesus was wrapped in burial clothes and wound through the town in a long procession, it was laid inside the cutaway rock tomb. Over the opening to the tomb a large rock was placed. It was one that had been especially carved and cut by a group of Italian stone cutters. It amazed the world that they had worked so fast in producing this beautiful memorial. It was flown in and placed.

Then the vigil began. Thousands and thousands of people took up every inch of space around the tomb. They were waiting for Easter morning. Jesus's adoring worshipers wanted to be there, because they believed, beyond hope, that he would once again rise from the dead.

***

I sat in my airplane seat, buckled in more by my total engrossment in the two books I had in my lap than the seat belt itself. In Revelation chapter thirteen and verse three, it says, "And I saw one of his heads as though it were wounded to death; and his deadly wound was healed, and all the world wondered after the beast."

What did that mean? Was the antichrist supposed to be killed and then healed of his head wound? Was it just a coincidence that the clone was shot through the head?

A few verses later I read, "...saying to them that they should make an image to the beast...and he hath power to give life unto the image of the beast, both to speak, and to cause that as many as would not worship the image of the beast should be killed."

There was that statue. But how in the world would they make it speak? Then it struck me. Thompson had been in love with the animatronics at Disney World when we were there. After that he'd done extensive research into how they were made, and was in contact with several of the top engineers around the world. He had another false prophet secret up his sleeve, and he was going to pull it out and display his magic for the world. This time it would be with a statue of Jesus.

Why hadn't I read this before? Why had I kept pushing the one source of truth out of my life? For the first time in years I closed my eyes, bowed my head, and began to pray.

"Father in Heaven, I can only express my deep sorrow for being a part of the horrible catastrophe that is coming to this earth. I did it because of pride. I did it for money, and because of all that, I deserve your punishment. I deserve to be judged for my crimes against you and all my fellow human beings. I know that I would be condemned before Your eyes for what I've done. How can I make things right? How can I gain your forgiveness?"

Tears swelled up in my eyes and I started to sob. If there was a Hell then I knew that God would have a special spot for me there. I couldn't imagine a much greater sinner than one who played god and created the being that would destroy the world.

After a few minutes, I opened my eyes and reached for a tissue to wipe my eyes. The Bible slipped off my lap and hit the plane's floor, and I reached over and picked it up. It had fallen open to a section, and I knew what it was…part of the Gospel of John, chapter three. I smiled. I could remember learning a verse when I was a kid…John three-something. Unfortunately, I couldn't remember which one, but my curiosity made me read to find it. I started to read.

"For God so loved the world that He gave His only begotten Son, that whosoever believeth in Him should not perish, but have everlasting life. For God sent not His Son into the world to condemn the world, but that the world through Him might be saved. He that believeth on Him is not condemned; but he that believeth not is condemned already because he hath not believed in the name of the only begotten Son of God."

Not condemned. Not condemned. Not condemned. That phrase reverberated in my mind. Not condemned. It was not the real Jesus's goal to condemn me. He came to save me. I didn't know how he had planned to do it, but I knew if I started reading I'd find the answer.

I paged through the Bible and the paperback book, trying to find guidance for my next step. No new direction came to me. I had decided to seclude myself in the mountains of California and keep my mouth shut.

After an hour I got up and went to the restroom. Upon returning I nearly walked by my seat because there was a man sitting in it, staring down at my Bible in his hands. I leaned over and tapped him on the shoulder. A sharp gasp slipped from my mouth. I couldn't believe who was sitting in my seat—CIA Director Jack Hesidence.

"Good reading here, Matthew. Did you discover what you were looking for?" he asked with a big smile spreading over his face.

"What are you doing here? How did you find me?"

"Sit down and I'll tell you all about it." I took the seat next to my original seat. "I was a little disappointed in you when you eluded my escorts in New York, but then I thought about it. Why in the world would you trust me? How do you know that I have your best interests at heart? So, I forgave your little indiscretion, but I also knew that I had to find you. I want the information that you're carrying."

"You're right. I don't trust you, and I'm not sure that I trust anyone right now," I answered, staring him right in the eyes.

"I can appreciate that. Now, I bet you're wondering how good ole Jack found you in Pittsburgh?"

"The thought did cross my mind."

"It's simple. We just simply fed your entire dossier, which is very large, into our computers. Then we matched up the news events, the names of the dead that littered the cities you visited, and voila! Out comes a plausible path for our fugitive. Now, the airport was an accident. I simply was flying in to pick up a fresh trail, and who did I see buying some books in an airport store?"

"What now?" I asked.

"That's up to you. I take it that you are meeting someone that I hope can hide you. The only thing I ask is that I know where you are. When you're ready to talk or I need information, then we'll connect. The rest of the time you can live as peacefully as possible. Maybe that way we can have a few less deaths in the country," Hesidence said. "You realize that just about everyone you've come in contact with is dead? Professor Grant gave his life to protect you. Your old school friend, Mary Grace, gave hers protecting your family. Then there's the priest in New Castle, and something tells me that you were involved with a now deceased police detective named Charlie Elliot."

"He's dead, too?" I slumped in my seat. Another person dead, and I seemed to be the one person connected to all of them.

"Now, your family is supposedly safe with some members of the dissenting church," he said.

"Supposedly?" I snapped.

"They're alive. My sources tell me it's with some of those church folk. She should be fine since your killers are right now searching all over Western Pennsylvania for you. By the time they would make it back to D.C. and flush out your wife, daughter, and grandkids, they should be with you." He stopped and looked down at the Bible, then continued. "I've been searching this book for some answers as well. Did you discover anything?"

"I'm not sure, but there is a reference to the Antichrist being killed by a head wound and then coming back to life," I said with a strange sense of excitement.

"Okay, so the clone is dead. How in the world are they going to bring him back from the dead? I heard there are thousands waiting around the rock tomb. They expect he is going to rise from the dead much like the real and Biblical Christ did. Is there any way it could happen?" he asked.

"Was he really killed or just made to look dead?" I asked.

"It was one of my men, Joshua Longtree, that caught the assassin. He was on the scene and verified the death. Actually, several doctors examined the corpse. He was dead all right," Hesidence reported.

"What did you say was the name of the guy who shot the killer?"

"Longtree, Joshua Longtree. Why? Does the name ring a bell?" he asked.

"I just heard Thompson talk about a CIA agent that he had some leverage with. I don't know more than that, but for some reason Longtree's name sounds familiar," I told him.

"Longtree had been assigned to watch over Thompson and Russo. I'm inclined to think that Joshua may be the one Thompson has under his thumb. No wonder he could never get me any damaging information on those two religious wackos."

"It all fits," I said.

"Yeah, except for one thing. How in the world are they going to bring him back to life? And if they do, then the three will be totally unstoppable," he said as he closed his eyes. I thought I saw a tear form in the corner of his closed lid, but Hesidence quickly turned his head away from me and stared out the window.

"What will happen if Jesus does rise from the dead?" I asked.

"I guess you didn't read the end of this book." He held up the Bible. "I've always had the bad habit of reading the end of the story before the rest of it. This ending is rather bleak."

"Armageddon, you mean?"

"That's only part of it. We will see a world war like never before. There will be plagues and earthquakes everywhere. Hell will have its day," he said.

"But did you see the real end of the story? Jesus, the real Jesus, comes back and wipes out the evil armies," I said as I pulled the Bible from his hands and flipped it open in his lap.

"But millions of people die in between. And all because one man—"

"Made a clone, I know," I said, with repentance in my voice.

"No, that's not it. All because I can't get the president of the United States to listen to reason and facts. He's had so many scandals in his administration he needs to look like he's on the side of goodness and decency. You won't see him making any moves against the Holy Army that Russo could put together if Jesus rises from the dead."

We both sat back in our seats and quit talking. When we did it was about families and sports. Neither of us wanted to think any longer about what we were involved in. Once the plane landed in Orange County, California we went our separate ways, after exchanging a private phone number that he gave me and an untraceable cell so he could get me when he wanted to. I expected to never see him again.

At the airport I was met by Sergeant Major Christopher Niles of the Pacific Protectorate, another underground dissenting group. Niles didn't ask a lot of questions. He followed orders and took me on a long drive into the mountains. We finally arrived at our destination on the outskirts of a very small town. Nine houses sat back on a mountainside cul-de-sac.

Once inside the safe house he brought in my luggage and another bag. He pulled the contents out and proceeded to show me each item.

"The general wants you to number one, die your hair. This packet will assist you in the project, and more can be purchased at the general store in town. He has also given you this laptop computer and small printer. The laptop has a modem set up to link into an absolutely secure system. You will send and receive email from this computer. But do not use your home phone. I suggest driving to a location about thirty miles due north of here and utilizing a pay phone. These clips and this instruction booklet will show you how to do it.

"The gun is a special issue. The bullets will pierce anything. Use it to protect yourself. You are far more valuable than any mistake you might make. In an absolute emergency, dial this number. Memorize it and destroy it. If we need to contact you, a neighboring soldier will contact you with this password; 'there's snow in Arizona.' We've also left a vehicle in the garage registered to one David Bunker. That is your new name. You'll find identification inside this wallet. My instructions are to leave you. May we be victorious," the sergeant said as he saluted me, spun on his heels, and retreated.

I looked at my watch and changed it over to California time. It was then that it struck me. In Israel the sun was getting ready to come up.

The dragon gave him his power, his throne, and great authority. And I saw one of his heads as if it had been mortally wounded, and his deadly wound was healed. And all the world marveled and followed the beast. So they worshiped the dragon who gave authority to the beast; and they worshiped the beast, saying, "Who is like the beast? ...And authority was given him over every tribe, tongue, and nation. All who dwell on the earth will worship him, whose names have not been written in the Book of Life of the Lamb slain from the foundation of the world. — Revelation 13

CHAPTER 31

Thousands of people kept watch near the tomb of my cloned Jesus. The sounds of the birds alerted them to the closeness of the rising sun. I tried to dial it in on TV, but no local stations carried the scene. It wasn't because they didn't feel it was newsworthy, but because the Prophet Thompson had declared it an exclusive media event for his network of cable stations. Everyone else was locked out. I switched to one of his stations and sat down to watch.

When I saw this something went off in my head. I was sure there was an event about to happen. Thompson could smell ratings, and I couldn't even imagine what advertising time cost.

I was watching the cameras trained on the tomb when suddenly into the screen stepped the prophet himself. "The prophet," I yelled. "That's it. There was the beast, the antichrist, and the false prophet. My God, we are really watching the beginning of the end."

Then Thompson spoke. "My dearly beloved flock, my heart is a mixture of intense emotions. Only a few short days ago I watched as the Prince of Peace, the leader of the world, the Messiah, Jesus, our lord, was shot to death. A gaping hole in his head allowed his life's blood to pour out. The scriptures saith, "Without the shedding of blood there could be no peace in the world.""

I flipped open my Bible and went to the concordance in the back. I found a verse similar to the one he quoted, but the reason Jesus shed His blood wasn't for world peace but for the forgiveness of sins.

"And I stand here like you would like to be," Thompson continued. "I stand here prayerfully hoping that the glorious sunrise will bring with it a new day, a new dawn, a new era, a new peace, a new government, a new world leader — the risen Jesus.

"We are only moments away. Could you all pray with me?" He paused, then began to pray in his preacher prayer voice. "Even now, come Lord Jesus!"

Blinding light filled the television. I could hear screams and Thompson was trying to talk. The lens readjusted to the light and I could see that the stone had rolled away from the front of the tomb. I breathlessly waited like all those watching around the world. Through the mist and early morning fog, a figure stepped from the rocky tomb. He was arrayed in gleaming white, and there seemed to be a backlit glow to his presence.

The cameras tightened onto his face. It was Jesus. It was definitely him. But he looked so much younger. So much healthier.

Thompson was watched by millions as he raced from his news reporter position and fell at the feet of Jesus. The Messiah pulled him up from the ground and spoke.

"I am risen. I have returned from the grave to rightfully take my place as the ruler of this world. I anoint the Reverend Thompson as my prophet. His word is my word. I also anoint the Archbishop Russo as the successor to Peter, the head of my church, the Pontifex Maximus."

I couldn't believe my eyes. In one minute's time Jesus had risen from the dead, made Thompson's word law for the whole world, and appointed Russo as the pope. My head dropped into my hands. I had just seen the fulfillment of the prophecies of the Book of Revelation. And I was the cause. I had brought about the end of the world. I wept. I wept bitter and hard tears for several hours.

***

In Israel the worshipers fell at his feet wherever he walked. They clamored to touch him in hopes that their diseases would be healed. Lame people were walking away whole. Blind people could see. I would have believed it if I hadn't seen the faces on a few of those miracle receivers. They were longtime Thompson employees, planted for the effect. Something stunk about what I was seeing, only I couldn't put my finger on it.

I sat and watched television most of the day until I heard a car pull into the driveway. I ran to the table where I had left the gun and grabbed it, then walked slowly to the window and peered out. It was Beth, Cari, and the kids.

I raced out to them and gave them all kisses. The soldiers ushered them into the house and opened special issue bags for each of them and gave instructions. Our new identities were in place and we were in our hiding place.

After they left I sat with my family and relayed the stories of my trip across Pennsylvania. Beth told me about Mary Grace's heroic act and how they were protected by the dissenting churches. She finished up with the tale of their trip to California.

Afterward, we ate and then Cari caught me alone and asked, "Dad, I'm really confused about this Jesus. If he is really not the true Jesus, then how did he resurrect from the dead? Not only did he resurrect, but he looks years younger. How? Why? Are we doing the right thing? Shouldn't you just give yourself up to the pope?"

"Cari, the clone's resurrection has me totally confused. I'll research my notes. I know there is something in them that will shed some light on this. As far as turning myself in…well, you know what they did to Mary Grace, Father Fred, and Professor Grant. They would do the same to me, your mother, you, and your kids. We'll be safe here as long as I don't release any more information. After all, Russo has the world's churches to run and Thompson has the world to run. I'll soon be forgotten."

And we were. For months we lived in peace as we watched the world move at a breakneck speed towards its own destruction. Diseases, famines, and plagues were gripping nation after nation. Each of them had to come to the Messiah clone and declare their allegiance and worship of him before their country could live in peace. I still felt safe in our little mountain top corner of the world. That was until the earthquakes came.

The one that has me presently trapped under the rubble of my former safe house came only hours after I called Hesidence's direct number. You see, I had finally discovered something that was tucked deep back in my memory and in my earliest notebooks. When I discovered it, I realized that I had the hidden secret that could end the madness of the false Messiah who controlled the world.

It was like a bolt of lightning hit me. The whole conversation and scene came flowing back to me.

"Doctor MacDonald, I'd like you to do one extra little thing for me," asked Father Russo. It was only days after I had successfully cloned the egg that became the Messiah.

"What is it, Father?" I asked.

"I have this great fear that I'm going to foul up this wonderful moment for both the religious and scientific world. If for some reason the egg is rejected by its surrogate mother, then we are fools before the world. I would like a little insurance against my own stupidity."

"You're right. We better have a contingency plan," I agreed.

"Please, make me a second egg. We will freeze it, and if there is a need for it then we can move quickly. If there isn't then I will destroy it right away," Father Russo promised.

A second egg. A frozen second egg that could be used to impregnate another surrogate mother a few years down the road. That Jesus could be brought up in total seclusion, and finally used at the most opportune moment. They had planned the assassination of the first clone all along. My news only made them quicken the pace of their plans.

Our new Messiah was simply a younger clone of my first Jesus. He wasn't resurrected. He wasn't rejuvenated. He wasn't even the Jesus clone that I knew. He was simply a carbon copy. I supposed that he was trained in seclusion for this moment as well. His arrogance and aggressiveness were untypical of even his predecessor.

My news would completely set Russo, Thompson, and their second clone back on their heels. No wonder he wanted me dead. I was still the only thing on earth that could stop them.

I had called Hesidence, then the quake had hit our area. My only hope is that he will find these pages when he arrives. I don't expect that he'll find me alive. I can feel the last of my life-force starting to slowly leave me.

I need to add one more thing. I did finally discover what the real Jesus meant when He said that He didn't come to condemn the world but to save it. I finally figured out how He saved it. It was that verse that Thompson quoted on his pre-resurrection show. "Without the shedding of blood there could be no forgiveness of sins." That was why He came. He came to die on the cross. His blood paid for my sins. I can go in peace knowing that in a few moments I'll be rejoined with my family and be in the presence of the real Messiah, Jesus Christ.

I'll put my pen down now. I hear something...the sound of shoes moving over the rubble along our street. I can't see who it is, but it sounds like there is more than one. I was right. There are two rescuers coming my way. I can see them now. They're getting closer. I can see their faces.

Oh my Lord! It's Russo's assassins. If they find my notes they'll destroy any chance of the world being saved.

They see me. Soteri is smiling as he moves right down to the opening I am watching him from.

"What's up, Doc? I bet you thought that you would never see us again. Well, since we ran out of friends and relatives to kill, we thought we might as well do you now. Say bye bye."

I heard a shot, then another. I expected to open my eyes and see myself in heaven, but I was still in my rubble prison and the bodies of my would-be assassins lay bleeding from powerful head wounds. Someone had ended their lives.

"Sorry it took me so long, Matthew, but the roads are a little torn up. But I made it in time to save your life," Hesidence said with a grim smile.

"Jack, I'm not going to make it much longer, but I've put everything you need to know in this manuscript. Take it and try to stop the madness I started."

POSTLOGUE

My name is Jack Hesidence. I'm the Director of the CIA. I took the materials from Dr. Matthew MacDonald and am preparing to give them to the president of the United States the moment my plane lands in Washington.

I am truly amazed at what is in these pages. Any person reading it would and could do only one thing— fight against the unholy trinity that has the world in its grip.

I dedicate myself and my duty to my country to do exactly that. May God forgive us for the sins we've committed.

SCRIBBLED AT THE BOTTOM OF THIS PAGE:
Henry,
Please have this document destroyed, and the news bearer as well.

Those words were penned by the president of the United States only minutes before he signed over the allegiance of this great country to the Messiah clone's One World Government. The president was last seen laying prostrate before Jesus, the God of this world, his prophet, and his priest.

Neither was the bearer of this document destroyed nor was this document destroyed. Although Henry, the president's aide, was. I have sworn to fight against the unholy allegiance. If you have read this, then you must make the same decision. Do you belong to Jesus Christ or to the unholy trinity?

Decide, then pass this truth along!

J.H.

Before You Go...

HELP AN AUTHOR
write a review
THANK YOU!

Share your voice and help guide other readers to these wonderful books. Even if it's only a line or two your reviews help readers discover the author's books so they can continue creating stories that you'll love. Login to your favorite retailer and leave a review. Thank you.

TIMOTHY W. AYERS

About the Author

Timothy W. Ayers is a retired pastor, recovering cartoonist and now full-time writer. After years of success writing bestselling Young Adult fiction, Rev. Ayers turned his attention to action thrillers. Utilizing his biblical training and strong network of authorities on his topics, Ayers writes fast moving stories filled compelling and believable characters that battle their fears, failures and faith. Tim now lives along the mighty Mississippi River where he is busy loving his grandchildren and working on his Lego building skills when not turning out new works.

www.ingramcontent.com/pod-product-compliance
Lightning Source LLC
Chambersburg PA
CBHW030252200626
46816CB00002BA/615